MW00526819

Salamandrine: 8 Gothics

Salamandrine: 8 Gothics

Joyelle McSweeney

Tarpaulin Sky Press
Grafton, vermont
2013

Salamandrine: 8 Gothics
© 2013 Joyelle McSweeney

First Edition, May 2013
ISBN-13: 978-0-9825416-9-2
Printed and bound in the USA
Library of Congress Control Number: 2012954372

Tarpaulin Sky Press
P.O. Box 189
Grafton, Vermont 05146
www.tarpaulinsky.com

For more information on Tarpaulin Sky Press perfect-bound and
hand-bound editions, as well as information regarding distribution,
personal orders, and catalogue requests, please visit our website at
www.tarpaulinsky.com.

Table of Contents

Welcome a Revolution

I heard you gave birth, that you named your kid for a star, but here you are with a beret, in charge of this cadre, and herding us into the basement of our building to be registered, photographed, and given new jobs to support the revolution.

It's pretty funny and you look great. You just gave birth but your skin is as supple and your eye is as bright when I saw you at that ~~party in February and you were six months pregnant~~, shiny hair, high heels, aqua scarf that matched your eyes, skin-tight black jersey dress hugging your "~~bump~~". Now even though you're running the show in the basement I'm close enough to you to see the wrinkles around your eyes and I wonder again how old you are like I did at the party and whether it was hard for you to get pregnant let alone get in charge of a cadre.

I think maybe you are going to get tired of me acting like friends with you while you're ordering everyone around. I'm not sure yet what kind of revolution this is, nor is anybody else. Is this the kind of revolution that likes or doesn't like intellectuals? And for how long? The only history I know is literary history and that does not have a nice story to tell about intellectuals and revolution. I wonder what to tell the guy with the computer when I do get to the front of the line and he asks me what I can do, what I can do for the revolution. That guy wears a trench coat and non-descript collared shirt and khaki pants, he looks like an IT guy, which is a kind of intellectual, I guess. He may actually be the guy who ran the tech at our Obama office last summer. Having tech in the Obama office gave us an invaluable, glamorous, indefatigable feeling, as we were told and believed that John McCain had no tech in his offices, even though our office was in Mishawaka, Indiana, a place that in no respect could be described as glamorous but in fact was the nadir of glamour, could strip a star of its glamour, just by sulking nearby.

The skills I can give the revolution include: writing, teaching, editing, and performing. Is that going to work? Good enough? Should I just say no skills, request training? I can't even cook, I can't watch babies or keep my car clean. Will you blow my cover? What answer do you want me to give?

The line is long and I'm at the end of it so I have a long time to think about the right answer. Because I feel so collegial with you I can't keep my mouth shut even when you're addressing everyone else in the basement. "I'm just excited about the career counseling!" I quip to the crowd, my neighbors, who laugh nervously. You also kind of laugh, but not deeply. How shallow or deep does it need to go in? Is laughter like a needle that can inoculate you, make me safe for you to have around? Is this that kind of revolution?

My mom is also here holding my baby, who's not really a baby anymore, she's two. If my mom's around I don't look after my baby too much. I wonder what my mom thinks of my baby-minding skills. Well, I don't have any baby-minding skills. I have art-making skills. Last week I did an art project with my baby instead of turning on the TV, which was like my new year's resolution for Spring. We dipped colored tissue in glue and stuck it to a card. It looked pretty excellent, like a garden, but when I put it on the wall she freaked out. 'No painting!' she whined until I took it down. She rejected the art we made together.

So where's your baby? I want to ask you but I don't. I want to joke, having a baby is like a reverse amputation, it's like a graft, like a protrusion. When I was a kid my brothers had these soldiers cast in some kind of metal, probably lead, they had a seam down their legs where they were made in the mold. That's what having a kid is like. Not the seam, but the soldier, made of toxic, and soldered to your mold.

Anywhere you turn they're lined up on the sill of your line of sight, with their sights on you, blocking your view.

Babies.

I don't say this because it's not strictly true, I don't see your baby anywhere, and I can only see my baby out of the corner of my eye in my mom's lap wearing a dirty white shirt and no pants.

I know, it's bad the kid has no pants but we had to come down here like immediately and what was I supposed to do? The revolution turned out to be like a tornado, for a couple hours we saw it coming, then it came, then we had to go down in the basement. It must be a pretty intense revolution if it has cells and cadres and chains that reach all the way out to Indiana.

And you look so glamorous here, again dressed in black, with your mascara and lip gloss, glowing like you're still pregnant, packing us all in, ranking and organizing us, and no baby in sight.

Everyone's staring at me, I feel like, because I'm not taking care of my baby, so I go over and grab her and plunk

her down in a corner where all the other babies are playing with toy cars, toy trucks, toy motorcycles. Every one
of these vehicles is plastic and red. Is it that kind of revolution—red? Or—plastic? Or—interested in transport?

When I saw you at the party I wasn't drunk despite my
best efforts. You looked so glamorous, you and your husband had been in Mexico and were buying a house in
Chicago, he was receiving serious accolades for a new
project based on erasure, but your own project was even
more interesting, a stack of index cards with typewritten
mottos, which were piled on a pillar in a plasticine box
and were taller than a stack of Russian novels, already.

Text was something that could be erased or accrue, and
it was really a material thing after all, and you could see it
build up over time like a coastline, or ebb away, and there
were kelp forests, deep water trenches, feeds of cool fresh
water that mixed up the bios, a shipwreck, canneries and
hotels and motels and whore houses and strip bars and
family aquariums that made a go of it and flourished for
awhile and fell into disrepair on the edges of it and finally sunk into the water itself to be reclaimed by the
kelp forest

was literature

in so many words.

Now I look down and that kid from school with the stringy blonde hair is about to bite my kid's arm in a fight over a toy so I pour my water on her head, and her mother comes over and grabs my wrist, and I pour out the rest of my water by accident on the floor, and now I'm worried, because how long are we going to be in this basement I should have saved my water. I look over and my mother is clutching a bottle of water and watching me, so, ok, she'll give that water to my kid before she drinks any herself, so I know the water thing is covered, I also look at you and you're drinking from a bottle of water and you hold your lips back a little bit so as not to get any lip gloss on the mouth of the bottle. I can see there's some flats of tiny water bottles behind you like at a youth soccer game. Are there oranges, too? Are those for the hundred or so of us down here or just for you and the cadre?

This does not appear to be an environmentalist revolution.

I knew your husband first, before I knew you, and actually before you knew him, I don't remember not knowing your husband, I can only imagine all the shit he's talked about me over the years, he's an inveterate gossiper and I love to hear gossip, though then I wonder what kind of gossip he's going to spread about me, of course I assume I'm boring, have nothing gossip-worthy for him to spread, but that's what everyone thinks, and my life is hardly perfect, for one I'm a failure as a mother and everyone knows that, partially because I tell them. Are you going to tell him, later, how uncool I acted at the revolution? Because I have been acting very uncool since this whole thing started, I agree. I was certainly acting very uncool at that reading party, you were amazing, magnetic, your bangs made a kind of shelving and I remembered how you had gone to a residency in the Canadian mountains somewhere, its name was onomatopoetic, I asked you, but I couldn't remember the right onomatopoeia, how was Wham, I asked, or Oof, is it, and you said gorgeous, gorgeous, I got nothing done but it was gorgeous.

I remember once we stopped to have lunch at your apartment while you were at work and we went in your husband's office, which was long and slim like a laundry closet or something, and we watched a little animation piece he was working on for a local band's video, which must have taken a ton of time and what's worth more, time or money? and I saw these books on anxiety disorder tucked up among his art books, so then I didn't know what that was, research for a project he was working on or did he have anxiety disorder, and he had photos around of when you two went someplace grey in the off season, Nova Scotia, but you didn't do any Elizabeth Bishop tourism, but the whole thing is Elizabeth Bishop tourism, stand with your toes in the marl and have a drink, the shoreline torn open by the storms like a fish's gut, noone could breathe inside this root cellar, sorry, wrong poet, wrong flavor of dread.

It is getting hard to breathe inside this basement, psychologically, at any rate, though I can hear a motor and the electricity is on and the airconditioning is keeping us cold as a catch, on ice, for what purpose.

Then I feel so bad for my kid and I take her in my arms and try to hold her close which she hates, she stretches her jaws to bite my shoulder, which she learned from that other kid, so I crouch down and release her and she toddles over to my mother.

You wouldn't know it, I say to you in my head, but at night she insists on me, she rolls over in her sleep and hooks an arm around my neck and knocks the air out of me, or if I'm sleeping on the floor next to her, she dive bombs from the bed to my chest, she lands on me heavy as reality and wakes me out of whatever dream I'm having, of an aerial bombardment or a revolution or whatever.

Your head turns back and forth, memorizing the crowd. Now I remember when your husband greeted me at that party and said, 'How's having a kid?' and I said, 'It sucks, don't do it' and he said, 'You know we're expecting, right?' and then I glanced over and saw you looking so beautiful in your blonde hair, seablue scarf, bump, and etcetera.

We both laughed as if it were an *urbane exchange.*

An *urbane exchange* does not a revolution make. Or?

Once when we were students you said you wanted to write poems like the *Sonnets to Orpheus.* Or was it the *Duino Elegies?* Either one seems a bit far fetched, not just for you but for anyone living in this century. Can you have a Rilkean revolution? Are you one of those instructors who assigns *Letters to a Young Poet* to your undergraduates? Who promotes the apprenticeship as a pedagogical mode?

The revolution is about apprenticeship, that much is true. All revolutions are pedagogical, that much seems sound.

Everyone is stepping into a little glassed-in office to give their information to the man with the computer, several at a time, they can't seem to restrain themselves, and really you're being pretty lax, and why shouldn't you be, we're not exactly an ornery bunch, women, children, older and younger men, none of us conducting our lives with much of a sense of purpose, most of us just anxious to see how this revolution is going to turn out, what is going to come next, and we're happy we're not out there in the elements being exposed to whatever was in that milky rain that showered the crowds we watched on TV. It put those kids to sleep right in the stadiums, and the cameras didn't stay on them long enough for us to know if they were going to wake up. Maybe the camera crews also passed out, they weren't in their bio suits just to cover the graduations that were naturally happening across the country this May weekend. Harvard, West Point, The University of Maryland, community colleges alike were hit with this milky rain that panicked those of us watching at home and caused us to just pull back and stay inside and out of it, out of it.

When you arrived to take charge of us, to tell us our part in it, we were relieved.

Finally I manage to get close to you and lean with my elbows against the wall. "I just can't believe you've been part of this revolution and having a baby at the same time! How long have you been involved in this?" I ask you.

"Eighteen months!" you say laughing.

"I just don't know how you get it all done! I'm so impressed! And you look great, I'm jealous!" I say, and mean it.

"Thanks!" you say. "But I'm still so fat, that's the one thing." Up close you look not quite as slim as usual, but, I know, the weight doesn't come off right away, and actually you look nice this way, you definitely aren't now nor were you ever fat, with your cheekbones and tiny ankles, I tell you.

"How old can your baby be, anyway?" I ask.

"Five weeks!" you practically squeal. Your lips are this gorgeous color like where liquor and liqueurs meet in a glass, and one of them is fruit, and I never order those, because all I can see when I look at that drink is spill.

"I love your lip gloss!" I say.

But what I mean, is, I love you! I love this revolution!

Mothers Over Lambs

Mothers over lambs, mothers before lambs. I arrived at a bureau office, which was a low cramped federal space. A door with vinyl numbers and with laminate which wore a federal blind. I had a seat in that place, I entered data, I had a calendar of the innocent species flipped to May, and in the waiting room on plastic chairs the populace was arrayed, each according to his entitlement, be it weighty or threadweight. I lowered my visor into the glare of the state, 'neath the lumen of its boniface, I pow'red up, til my legs did vibrate, and on the meadow-yellow screen, I saw rules writ, I saw blinking numbers split and clasp to make screen music, clots of script sticking to the screen through the day which when rebooted, was erased, but when collected, ciphered this, which I did print:

Mothers over lambs, mothers before lambs
Knives before trees
Wire up on wire
Brick upon brick
Falls before breeze
Fist before palm
Wrist before fire
Fire before lamb
Last fire before flame
Dawn before break

Break before break of dawn
Burst before wake
Balm before break
Wrist before fire
Fire before lake

Burst before dam
Mothers before breath
Mothers before sheet
First burst before weak
First blood before wind
First blood before wake
First blood before wire
Mothers before lambs
Wind before world
Blood before wake

I took these several sheets and wrapped them in a folder, I took the folder and placed it in a binder, I did take of that binder and place it in a tote, I did take of that tote-bag and place it in a wheelie, I did take of that wheelie and jam it with other files, I did pull that wheelie out to my hatchback, I did drive in my hatchback to my apartment block, I did climb the exposed stairs to the second level, I did bounce each cement step with my holy burden, I did arrive at last at the second level, I did study my door with its swart eye and knocker, a knocker like a second eye which did stand for vision, for it was gold and shaped like both a mouth and an eye, for there is only one eye which both casts and receives vision, for he is the LORD, for his offices are in the highest, for however the LORD does not speak English, for however he does not choose to speak it, for however the software operated in my office appears to operate in English, for however it pleaseth the LORD to conform to the software which he himself also designed and implanted in the mind of mortals, for they are IT consultants who did receive the government contracts, for they shall be held as favorites and made wealthy in man's eyes, for the code of the government is on their shoulders.

I did enter into my apartment with its shag carpet, which was burnt in places like an incomplete offering.

There I sat on my couch and removed the sheets from the file from the binder from the tote from the wheelie. I spread the sheets on the smoked glass table and did further read:

Mothers over lambs, mothers before lambs
Gilt before birth
Birth after afterbirth
Dream after afterlife
No birth without death
No lamb without mother
No word without fire
No fire without knife
No blood without lamb
No lamb without mother
Mothers over lambs, mothers before lambs

Then I got on my knees, clasped knuckles, and praid, and I praid with tears in my eyes, because the LORD had chosen me, but also because he had chosen me for his most terrible vision, Mothers before lambs, a hardening of soft and the supple now turned to childish throats. Poor harmless species, now come to harm. I prayed and prayed to the LORD, thanksgiving and guidance, thanksgiving and guidance, and when I was exhausted of prayer I slept, and when I awoke with my cheek in the carpet, I saw streetlight fingering a woven drape at the window, and when I went and looked out the window, I saw people moving dimly in the night, out of their apartments, mothers in shirts that strained at their breasts, strained at their shoulders, babies in Pampers and nothing else, and other children on bikes who wore huge white shirts like ghosts, and they moved in an out of the vague light, and their shirts did hang about them, and they were less definite than the light, like stranded spirits, and I knew it for a vision, because I knew from the news it was a cold cold night.

*

The next day was a work day but I was afraid to do my work, I was afraid what the screen would show me. Oh how sinful and how cowardly, truly was I that day, lower than a snake, vain species. I sat before my screen but did not pow'r up, and so I saw only my own face like a drowned fish's in the glass, like a stubborn fish that refuses water, for it sees not, for its eye and its mouth are both empty. From time to time I retreated to the washroom, and looked on the large plastic cleaning cylinders arrayed in clean ranks, dull white with bright pink writing, bright as eyebright, as the ill-eyes of snakes, as the myxomatosis that brings low the rutty hare, as the eye of every haunched and wriggling thing: rat and mouse and stoat and ferret and eagle and ermine, which during

~ 16 ~

a recent birdplague did lie sluggish in fields like a robe
for Queen Carrion, I saw this on the cable news which
has as its symbol the eye of the carrier pigeon, which carries its eye like a wheel within wheel, an eye which could
hold a scrolled map of the world, or hold it wired to its
spurred ankle, and which is extinct, and of the growwort
which brings down the vain stand of lilies, which wear
the blush of rot in their face, and shall be vanquished,
as pink as flux, as inflammation, as pink as inflammar-
ion, little slipper that sluffs the vein, plaster, plaque that
phlubs the wall of the eye till pressure bursts it, pink as
lung or brain, an infected catharsis or vain invention,
pink as an Easter leukocyte, as pynk as eyester, then I
did feel a pilgrimage in my veins, a desire to flow to the
broad place and the narrow, the high place and the low,
to show what a wide place is the mouth of the needle
for one so humble, so meek mild, for one who takes dic-
tation, and what a wild place is the marrow of she who
near succeeds. For future shares a shelf with failure. Thus
the pink writing strummed up a keen relentless musick,
pricking and pure, like a gas of particulates it did lodge
in each pore of me and lift me as a fume from that place.
Then I did return to my desk with renewed vigor and
purpose, and pow'red up. From the next desk a red plastic radio did hiss songs of crudenesse and seduction but
I was as cheerful amidst this as a wax martyr among
flames: how soon it would melt, how soon the earthly

matter would be put aside and away. Before me sat three children, of which one was the mother. She pushed her papers across at me and looked off. Her hair was a dried blonde like fishtank water, like the amber lives of exemplary fish, their faith, their uprightness. All three children wore jackets that bulged at the middle and were too short for their wrists, and had enormous hoods which propped up their limp heads. The mother had skin of a sickened cue ball, its slick, and the children had browner. On each jacket was a gleaming zipper which flexed its teeth and flashed one eye like a snake in profile in triplicate it rolled its gap eye at me and bit its own teeth like: *I'm biding my time*. Then I held my breath between my teeth and breathed 'bless you, bless you' as I typed the information from the form to the screen, which made a rhythm, then I handed the papers back and said "six to eight" and the mother child said "but I need it now" and I handed her a pamphlet. "How do I get there?" she asked and I handed her a bus schedule with the temporary bus pass and was counting "bless me, bless me" to end on an even number not an odd and she was erased.

Then again sat a mother before me and her hair was scraped straight back on her head and her head was small as a gymnast's with a gymnast's small ears full of holes and one hole tore clear through and she wore an red satin athletic jacket large enough for a man. She had her child who was a grown man though could you call him a 'grown' man he had grown to the size of a man and then shrunk like a saint within a metal frame and a straw to speak through. "Holy, holy, holy" I said with a half a breath and the saint's eyes watched me. She took out the papers she had all the papers with her in a Looney Tunes child's school folder soft and split white at the seams the Tazmanian Devil danced on it it was in the computer now and the data danced verdant on the screen, like a Springe that has come into blackness, yea, and the data danced in an imageless program and there it was revealed that he was a saint by motorcycle accident oh LORD you work in pretty obvious ways for those of us who know how to look at it maybe the motorcycle came out looking perfect was it hawked bartered sold for junk or battered apart by the saint's cousins after his back-from-rehab party on a freezing January night before his granddad died and noone had known where the kids had got to then the next morning if raccoons could tear apart a motorbike oh it's a shame it could a been sold to someone who would want it jinx bike well the parts will sell anyway to the junk man and in another day they were gone.

Then sat two men who had been Marines but that was years and decades and now they were so weatherworn they couldn't sit upright or even shoulder to shoulder. One pushed a cassette into the other, lifted the phones to his own ears, where they sank into his wavy greased black hair, like a stilled unparted sea, or upturned earth, black soil, and then his eyes spread, as if he was shocked at what his ears told him, though it had been his own choosing. The other sat with the player in his lap smiling nervously and listening to nothing.

Mothers over lambs, Mothers before lambs. Then I sat at the light, the ground kept turning cold and hot and murked the light, big grey piles of plow snow that looked like lint, held together with radio static, which did flex and go dim as I drove from light to light, and here the snow hemmed in a lot of cars, and men in black jackets were entering and leaving the pawnshop with nothing in or on their hands like a magic trick where you finish where you have started. Then I was going the other way, and I saw a man and a woman in sweatsuits lugging a window air-conditioner towards the locked door of the shop, and they saw that it was locked and set down their load like a fever, beside the bales of snow, and they were sweating cold, and they looked worriedly through my windows and past me to the office of the Wooden Indian, which was a motel turned inside out, a kind of motor court, with almost no inside to it, as if they were worried someone would look out and see them, if they had also stol'n it from the store-rooms of the manager, I couldn't say though I am well acquainted with the world's wickedness.

And then days and nights safely in my apartment in the world going hot and cold with fever, because of our situation on a lake. I recall the lake in hell to which Jesus was chained, though the devil couldn't lick him. The weather here is that kind of strait. On the news there are sister-brother anchors and they attempt to be helpful both with fine brown heads of hair they could probably do anything with but they wear it slightly puffed on top as helmets under the studio lightings and they go on reading what's on the screen before them like it was scripture and they were the most innocent species reciting the LORD's life for the multitude it's serious now listen to the LORD area food banks are suffering sales at the shopping mall no jobs for young people, old people, or any people but good news our wild weather will settle down by Monday in time for the morning commute.

I took out the Bible and the Yellow pages the line-art woman in her wedding veil her doctor's coat her styled hair her just-washed car, demonstrating earthly fulfillment at the hands of local merchants, also mortal, and clarity of line. Goods and services made of dust. Then I unfolded my own text, which I had prepared, Mothers over lambs, mothers before lambs read my sampler made with a stencil from Dollar Tree, then the numbers backwards from nine and the leftover elements of the alphabet.

I belted my coat around me which left me thick as a charger of the LORD though for a lance I had only my purpose. As I walked my breath curled around me as if I myself were a painting of the demon and saint. I had been an innocent species but the LORD had loved me to make me his Discerner. St.Bavo and St. Hilde, St. James the Less, and the Church of Old St. Mary, a congress of churches like a holy war. But my building was almost under an overpass which lept up to connect the river to the city field. So there was no church near me except two days a week a storefront River of Life. I peered into the dusty glass and saw nothing in the darkness but the streetlights behind me and then the lights over the river and beyond that the stunted airport and beyond that the lake and blackness all the way to the chancred megacity.

Mothers over lambs, mothers before lambs, for, Lo, I continued south, where the employment office sat like an empty box in the middle of an asphalt lake. It had a glass vestibule where a young man sat, and seeing me he stood up to his full height, he seemed taller than the building, and looked right at me but saw me not, and he was clad in the bluest raiment like a queen and like a mother, and it was blue and clean, and it draped away from him in large folds so elegantly and so serenely, and his face was not serene, he wore a sleeveless jerkin and large shorts, and his socks and his sneakers were a dazzling white, and on his chest were two numbers, and as I approached him with my flagwork, he waved me away and turned from me, I read on his back one word: JORDAN, crystal river, singular reason, dividing line, marking the edge of foster-age, and he was standing there like a sanctity, a messenger of the LORD, and the phone he had about him did ring with petitioners, and he began to speak in laughter, but he would not consider my petition, and he did not want me to approach him, though he was wearing the mother's color, and Mothers before Lambs, Mothers over lambs.

For angels have no sex, and are therefore male, and are very tall, and thanking the LORD for this vision though he would not admit me for angels are not all-knowing they only carry knowledge from the LORD I turned my back on him and was warmed by my own knowledge and returned to the steps of my building and was lifted up.

*

The next day His offices were closed and above me the white ceiling a hole had opened there.

It was a perfectly round hole that seemed to have breath-ing edges. The surface of the hole that was moist and black. It could not have opened in the night except by the finger of an angel tracing it there my communicant.

For I had slept in my coat for warmth and now as I began to rise from the bed I was glad I had this to protect me from this slick material.

I did hear a ringing then like money in the bank. I was in a bankvault with a gryphon and sphinx, both were executives, with briefcases locked to their wrists, and they bent their bodies to fit the giant vault, and their shorn heads brushed the flat gold ceiling, and I was pressed up against their pinstriped haunches, the long sweep of a lion's-wing, heavy as gold cloth occasionally brushing the ground next to me, and each beast was several stories high, so that I could barely look up and see the horned chin of the gryphon, the lovely chin of the sphinx, and both chins were moving very fast as if they were praying, bartering or gobbling something, and the gold-coin music was thick in the air around my ears, like an elevator continuously arriving at its floor, but my nose and mouth were full of dander, which was sun-warmed but also smelled of meat, and I could not breathe around it but gagged, and I did swoon, and when I awoke I could not see, for mine eyes were thick with congealed blood, but did receive this further vision: lambs dashed in a field, red coated, red dye on eagle's talons, red dye surfeiting a woman's teeth, her lips split, a red satin jacket struggling over eagle's wings, and sweatpants stuffed with lion's haunches, and then I could see, and I could see through the walls of my apartment to a populace hunched and sleeping or feeding on carrion lamb, a populace of sick-gutted beasts.

OH LORD, your city of species.

*

The next day His offices were closed and I stayed in the house and did PRAY and I did watch the morning, lunchtime, and evening news and the morning and afternoon talking programs and all the anchors with their gilt hair and closely cut clothing did speak to me with their eyes as their mouths addressed other matters and they did smile constantly and tell me to be watchful so I did watch all that day but no further visions.

That night I again left the apartment I had become nocturnal like a golden bat or mechanical owl who leaves his pocket watch cave I did move through the streets I did see a man with a shopping cart of pipes and flashings I did see another man with a cart and the two men also caught sight of one another in the middle of the street they did remove from their carts each a solid pipe they did hit each other about the shoulders, waist, and ears with these pipes until at last one man fell down in the street and the other man made off very slowly with both carts though only for a few feet it was too heavy so eventually he did push off with just his original cart.

Then I did approach the man in the street who had a heavy blow over one ear blood and matter I did not look close for there was a kind of summation in that appearance the blood face which is the true face on earth so it was already known to me I said holy holy and returned to my home for this was enough for one vision.

*

The next day His offices were opened and I did see a Mother with racks of raiment laid in the back of her pickup truck. She did exit her truck and bring the rack of clothes into A + J Resale, and she did return with the clothes before the lights could change. They were ironed so stiffly that I could make out each button and seam and the cut of them from where I sat and it made me wonder if like a nocturnal thing my eyesight were getting sharper or if like a nocturnal thing I could now see through all my organs of sense my skin my ears my tongue, and all is sight.

But then no for other times I was seized in a kind of senselessness and was sev'ral minutes lost to myself and late returning from my lunch half hour. At such times I wondered if my nerves had suffered from a surfeit of sense.

*

My co-worker Deirdre was another Christian and she had made a project of me clearly she recommends vitamins and even bought me a small package which sits on my desk small and irradiating a smug expiration date a concern with flesh vain species but I did put one in my mouth at her urging and then I spat it to my hand and ran to the washroom and rinsed my mouth at the faucet and did look on the white containers and read their repetitive scripture, from container to container.

Another time she did join hands with me and a few others of the workers before our shift and we did pray to the LORD about serving out our shift in a spirit of gratefulness and saying a preliminary Thank You to the universe for all the bounties that had and would be shared with us and I stood there with righteous anger in me for what will be given to she who is afraid to read the messages given to her and she who will stop searching for the time at which to act and the method in which to act Mothers over Lambs Mothers before Lambs.

Then again she did ask me since I was a Christian also would I like to volunteer at an Christian education program for children whose parents worked evenings and could not provide them with Christian education at that hour.

Then I did feel a kind of sharpness under every finger-nail, as if there were a talon growing there, and a tough-ness as of a horny plate at my knee, and I did feel my shoulderblades shift to a new purpose, and I did acqui-esce, and I went again to the washroom where I did see a thick golden mask upon my face, a browpiece folded in stern furrows, a hooked and ferocious beak, and though it was all of gold it was not heavy, as if it were also of fire, it burned and purified the air. And when I turned my head I caught in profile the face of a beautiful and wise Mother, made of wax, fastened at the ball of my skull with bolts, and her hair was shaped and fixed in rows like circuits, and she held knowledge there, and I knew then that though I had been an innocent species I was now refit to the purpose of the LORD, and to his instant, I would be a less humble species, but not a vain one but one who was like unto a machine of the LORD, a lion, eagle, mother, and could not but be his machine.

Mothers over lambs, mothers before lambs. With great concentration I fit my lion's haunches to the flimsy desk chair, kept my wings from ramming the soundproofed ceiling or puncturing the tiled floor. It was all as nothing, and to keep within it took a focus of will. My forehead was ringletted with information, and information was mapping itself into the neurons and dendrites with which my wings were wired, and all motions programmed into my muscles, and my muscles changed with knowledge. At first human voices were too quiet for my ears and I relied on the papers they thrust at me, papers that anyhow were as definite as the fates in describing their mortal futures. When I gazed onto the vernal screen before me, an innocent species of knowledge spread mildly in its beauty, and for the first time I felt my gaze as an instrument which could go out as well as recede, though it could change nothing it touched, but it could touch, and it could know also, and this was a gift the LORD had granted me, for complying with his will.

Then I was no longer sexed but was a MOTHER.

And out in the parking lot I saw a male in a thin striped cotton shirt hunched over his steering wheel spasm as if vomiting and I knew him to be a MOTHER stripped by the world poor mother.

For those who would be improved or undone by the LORD are called MOTHERS and those who are sent by the LORD are called angels I cannot phrase it more plainly than that.

At home in my apartment I did also begin to spasm or shiver and I thought if I am now MOTHER and a new species can I also have a virus in my flesh for my new flesh did not feel natural nor did my hunger nor did my heat. But then a virus can only spread from like to like species or cross between species and I did not know any contact with another like or unlike myself except in a dream did look on a gryphon and a sphinx. Nor could I recall the day of my birth when such things may have been communicated nor did I any longer have a birth as I was a MOTHER now and am not born, nor can die, I suspect, though the LORD has not revealed it.

Then I did turn on every light in my apartment, every appliance, the radio, the oven, I opened the refrigerator and ran the taps and in that flowing thawing box I did feel relieved of the heat and weight of my gold raiment and I did feel clarified and did see.

There was a MOTHER sitting opposite me who did have in her lap a pile of mail paper envelopes with plastic windows. And the male was crossed on her lap and did have a shattered appearance and was paperwhite or like a lamb did bleed instructively, and his head was pierced to let the visions out which did spread maternally or bead inscrutably on his plated forehead. She did smile noncommittally as in a waiting room and she did not provide a message for me but just went on reading her mail and making piles in her lap which was perhaps what she was meant to instruct to me good MOTHER. And then I did look at my own lap which was piled with mail, and the mail did not have a bill nor a check nor did request payment but was merely printed with information, and when the mail was removed from each envelope then the plastic window did provide a vista on its own lining only and did not cast or receive vision.

*

The next day I did dress myself in a pink garment printed with innocent species and invoking Springe which is the time of lambs Mothers before Lambs.

And I did feel the workday race and held onto my workspace with white knuckles and did say 'bless me, bless me' in counts of onehundred as one might on a diving plane, not a prayer for deliverance but a prayer to bless my mission this night and all the missions for which it might please the LORD to program me. It was five o'clock in one mortal interval and Deidre did gather a pale coat about herself and gesture to me. We did stop for fast food where although I could taste nothing I suppose I ate voraciously as Deirdre again and again commented the speed at which I consumed the meal. But though I could not taste the stuff in my mouth or even feel it each bite did empower me and eventually I stood up still partly bent to the plate and chewing and Deidre was pleased by my haste to do the LORD's work to which I said Amen, Amen.

As we walked into the dusking night the sky also made a chamber red and purple pooling at its base and a glistening black at its vault. For I believe we were in a not-quite-mortal space but inside the heart of a brave and beautiful species that was however nearly dead, or inside some other organ, perhaps inside its eye.

And all was slow and could dilate there, after the brevity of the mortal day. So for some centuries we stood with a foot on a cracked concrete step as Deirdre blew smoke into the night, an offering, and insects, armored, resourceful species, moved over this step as over a corpse. Then we did enter the church building, which was the building of the school. We walked to the furthest classroom and an array of small children, four and three. I studied their dirty faces. Some had the dullness of goats, and others had a cat's brightness. They were of an unknown species which was not innocent though it could not think; instead it was wholly given over to desires. This species must have sprung from that minx Eve before she even got the fruit in her mouth. I felt the weave of my muscles tighten just looking at them, my wings shift in readiness. Then one coughed, and like a signal, all coughed. One snickered and all snickered. Deirdre led them in 'Yes, Jesus loves me', then handed me a bag of loose flat beads, and I moved among them doling out and studying the shape of each face, the sharpness, bluntness, blankness of each gaze. Then she handed them out each a card. She said that the beads were the LORD's heavenly treasure in which he had entrusted them at birth, or even before birth, when they were in their mommy's tummies, or even before. The card was printed with a grid of sins. As Deirdre drew sins from a hat and explained what each meant each child was to cover up that sin with a bead. It was like Bingo but bending towards obscurity. A life totally blotted out by sin, which was just. Though these children perhaps because they were stupid as goats or drugged or demented with lead didn't follow the game but merely applied the beads at random or stacked them in different patterns. One child licked one and adhered it to his forehead, and then all the other children tried to make theirs adhere.

And then, while Deirdre was frowning over the instruction sheet and I was studying the children, the miracle happened.

One child slipped a bead into her mouth, her glassy colorless hair falling back from her neck as she shook her head to swallow it.

Then each child selected a bead, and swallowed it, their necks bulging with the effort.

Then the girl selected another bead, and put it in her mouth, and did choke on it.

Then each child put a bead in his mouth and began to choke. Some merely pretended to choke until they were choking. Some thrust themselves against their desks unconsciously and gagged the beads back up. Deirdre did look down at the room full of foaming, gagging, and shaking children, and began to scream, running from child to child and punching them in the gut. I also ran from child to child and punched each in the gut. She stopped what she was doing and screamed at me, her own eyes rolling in her head, her mouth foaming. "Call someone!" she beseeched me. There was a phone on the wall of the room, and I did go to it, and did dial up the earthly authorities as the room began to smell of sulphur and the first child stopped moving.

Then as I studied the room it seemed that four children had survived and these children were crying or vomiting, and it did seem that six children had choked and these children were dead.

And then these dead children all sat up straight backed at once and each had a gold coin in his mouth which shone light from it and shot light back up through their eyesockets. Small gold stunted wings like doorknockers crabbed at each shoulder.

Each did fly shoulders first like dry cleaning sliding forward on a rack to where I stood with my hand on the phone. Each did like a bird spit the gold coin into my hand. 'Bless me, bless me' they sang in mocking aria, circling, as the spit-covered boluses piled up in my palm. I did not look down at the six boluses as I was sore afraid. Then each thrust out a tail, and each did swallow his own tail lasciviously, and each did make a kind of spinning blade and split the floor and dial down to Hell and the room did seal up after them where they had left their mortal bodies.

I put the boluses into a pocket just as the ambulance drivers in their coats entered the classroom which was too small for them these men were big even in their mortal bodies the children were too small for the gurneys they did not have ten lamb-sized gurneys for the living and the dead children and had to make calls on their instruments which were coloring the sacred air grey with static.

For then I realized that there was a gilding to the air that rang as if struck. For I did ring and strike the air, and the air smoked with the LORD's gladnesse.

The Bottle

It's Tuesday afternoon and the weather's asleep with its belly and long tail wrapped around the town. The curtains are hot with it.

I'm writing this yesterday.

I was going to write this from a distance, like I was God studying the classified ads of this town, old God scowling through his magnifying glass, God with long breaks for the bathroom, God sweating it out in polyester pants with the doors and windows locked against tweakers and Mexicans. God before he comes back in the second half as a long-haired teenager.

When we moved into this house the door was hanging from one hinge but the other side was heavy with bolts and chains just brushing the floor uselessly and the frame was busted. Someone had tried but couldn't lock someone out. We stayed at my grandma's til June, then moved after school ended. School's important to Ma. But that means we showed up here with nowhere to go, all day not knowing anybody. Ma works the halfday at Target and half as a checker at Martin's and most nights she brings something home from the half-price barrel: hot dog buns, marshmallow fluff, Miracle Whip a day or two off. And you have to wait a long time for Miracle Whip to go off. I'm sure Noah took it with him in the ark, it's that practical. Maybe even this very same jar.

And he didn't even have to wait in the ark that long. Not as long as summer vacation. And he had all the animals to talk to, though it must have smelled bad.

When school starts we'll get folders from Target, nice ones this year. Me and Tasmin already have ours picked out.

But then there's the bottle. It's thick like a jar with a big cork on the top. Moonshine maybe, Ma thought. We left it up there; it was too heavy to move. Just a couple of inches of liquid in the bottom that you couldn't tell what color it was supposed to be. The house also came with the pullout couch where Ma sleeps, the thin beds where Tasmin and me sleep, and a chest of drawers. So except for the door, it's nice here, and a man from church came and fixed the door and also hooked up the electric to a wire outside.

Tasmin disappears every morning before I can barely wake up. Tasmin's mean, which is lucky for her. Meanness is like a magic charm. It makes you hard, and hardness protects you. That's obvious. That's in any book (except the Bible). Tasmin is also half black, which is weird, because she's blonder than me, I mean her skin is blonde, and even her eyes are kind of blondey green. My hair and my skin are like soap or a dishcloth or anything plain you'd find around the house.

She's eleven and I'm thirteen.

I started it with the bottle. When I had looked at everything a million times, I sat on the couch and stared at the bottle up on its shelf until the air went thick between us. Then, inside the bottle, the liquid went a little thick and bulged. It sent up a bubble. I was so surprised I made a little noise out loud, it just bubbled out of me, and then the noise surprised me too. Suddenly the house felt so still and quiet I went out on the concrete and sat down. It was too hot for my bare legs. A bird was hopping around like the concrete was too hot for its feet. It kept turning its ear to the ground. It's supposed to hear worms that way. Living under the concrete, under the ground.

The next day after Ma and Tasmin cleared out I returned to the exact same spot on the couch and studied the bottle. It seemed a little fuller now. Sunlight was hitting it from somewhere high up, and the light hit little gold flecks and grains suspended in the liquid, which was now a definite green. The specks swirled around like dust swirled in the air. They swirled around and then spread out and then clenched back in again. Like something that lives deep in the water and not in a bottle on a shelf. It repeated this motion and repeated it. It was getting organized.

Then there was a knock at the door. It was the guy from church who fixed the door up in the first place. Steve he reminds me. How're you doing sweetheart? He says Hoo it's pretty hot in there you should keep this open.

He comes in and sits on the couch. I also sit on the couch and keep my side to the bottle so I don't have to watch it, but of course that side of my face feels fat and hot. He's talking about this and that, I don't know what, his own daughters, they live with their mama too up in White Pigeon. He bought this for one of them but it was too small, they've grown up so fast, what do you think, sugar?

He says and he pulls out of this paper bag (I didn't notice before) a hot pink t-shirt. That gets my attention. It's printed with a shower of stars down the front, and the bottom is all fringed and fixed with beads, and instead of sleeves it has a knot on each shoulder and a couple of beads dangling from there too. He lays it flat on my lap. I pull at the beads. He asks why I don't try it on. Then something jumps up in my throat from my stomach, I don't know what, but it feels round and golden, and I can barely make a breath around it, but finally I gasp out Tomorrow, I'll try tomorrow and he pats my knee. He says, alright then, sweetheart, I'll be by tomorrow, and I'll bring some Cokes. But put that special shirt away, don't let your sister or your mama know about it, that's just for you. And that's it he's gone out the door.

My heart is beating like a rotten pond, like what's in the bottle, and my ankles are shaky when I get to my feet. I don't look at the bottle, but now's when I hear it knock. Or is that just my heart, trying to shake me, trying to beat me up from the inside? Why is my heart mad at me? Why is the bottle? I don't want to look. I feel like just looking would hit me in the face.

But I run to our bedroom and I try on the shirt. It's all spangled and reflects light. It hangs down my chest like a shield with hearts. I wear it for a while, and then I stuff it way down between the sheets in my bed. Then I lie on my bed for the rest of the day, until I hear Tasmin bang in.

And then the next morning I put on my shirt and sit on my bed as the silence in the house goes all thick. I pull my hair back on top which makes me look older. Sunlight cuts in the dirty windows and the curtains too. Dust swirls around the light like it can't get satisfied. I wish I had my ears pierced and some earrings.

I'm listening but I don't hear the knocking of the bottle just something that taps in my own head quiet and steady like Tasmin messing with me trying to make me mad. I feel a little mad. My madness is small like a little fire made of the points of needles, a gold fire like I've never seen. I pick it up and it tinkles like a chain. I tie the fire around my throat and it goes inside and makes a weird fat ring under the skin. It holds my neck up and my chin up pointy and stiff like a princess's. I stand and walk all slowly into the next room. My t-shirt is gone and my gown is hanging down all around me yellow and heavy and my neck is bulging. The next room is full of a yellow light. It's coming from the middle of the room. There's a huge yellow glow there, and floating in the middle of the glow is a yellow lizard and a yellow baby. They're the same person. His tail bends forward under a pair of stunted little baby legs with claws that crab the air. There's a rash of pale yellow bumps up the back of his tail. His big baby belly's like a frog's belly I can see a vein in and two little arms just lie on the belly, and then there's his huge head like something came out of the oven wrong, the part that holds the brains is all piled up on the forehead in a big folds, and his head's so heavy his neck bends forward in a curve, and there's a slick of yellow pond slime over the eyes. He sneezes and I can see he has these wounds on both sides of its heads like three slashes healing over. Who cut this big messy baby? It's not a cute baby but it's helpless like a rotten onion.

Then there's a knocking, knocking, knocking at the door and I run for the baby. When I reach him I'm instantly dirty from my hair to my feet in a cold and sticky muck. All I can see is glow so I wave my arms around crazy and feel for the baby. The baby's laughing in my ears like nickels but I also hear the knocking knocking and I know it's Steve. Coming, coming! I say but already my feet can't move and I'm feeling around my knees for the baby, is he hiding there? Coming, coming! I say but I can't bend down any more, just stick my arms straight out and move them in circles, hoping to catch at the baby. Coming, coming I try to say but the glow stuffs my mouth and it rings like nickels. Then I feel something press at both my ears and wrench my neck and face towards the door. Pond scum stretches from my eyes to the door, and then it burns through the door to where Steve is standing with a nice smile on his face. Then my eyes burn out his smile and his face falls away and I can see his skull and his teeth smiling like on a poison bottle and I know that's a message for me. Then his collar's on fire and a little bit of the tree branch that was hanging over his head and then the skull starts shaking in midair and I can see his spine like a stem flexing in the fire of his shirt and it sways and it sways and then it collapses in a pile and the fire snuffs out instantly though this sour smoke is rising neatly and symmetrically from the little pile in all directions.

Then all of a sudden I can move again and my old mad feeling comes back and it's shaking inside of me like a million gold chains and all the words come into my head that Tasmin calls me when Ma's not around. I fly to where the door used to be. I look down on this pile of ash and dirt and I just start pounding it with my feet. Steve you motherfucker, Steve! What did you do to the door, Steve? Steve you slut asshole. What did you do to the *door?* Then I go in and fill up the spaghetti pot with water and come back and dump it on the step and the little pile is gone though the step is streaky black. Then I keep doing it until this streaky black is gone.

Then I go back and sit on the couch. The door is gone except for the knob and hinges which sit on the ground, but I don't look at them. I'm looking at the shelf, where the bottle used to be. Now with nothing on it. My sexy t-shirt is gone too, burned off me, and I can feel a breeze on my bare skin, and a breeze inside, too, a kind of rising. Where the baby's gone, where the baby's going to be.

Salamandrine, My Kid

1. The twittering machine lies in its crib, rehabilitating its connections. It nails up its habitation, darts up its habillement, it letters its joints, limbs, pistons, limpid injectors for easy filling stations, for stations of, for remote and E-Z filing. It files under 'pay'. It flies by night. It learns by rote. It rotors. It knocks the bars into its head.

It crawls out of the snake grass, snuckering.

It crawls out of the camera.

It pads the walls of the retinal box: remember?

2. I'm crawling over the carpet to demonstrate a torpedo roll. My kid hoists her kid belly like eightmonths of night-shifts she's a kid Demosthenes and the pack of dalmations is snapping at her back. The episodic ice floes flow. Amid a mouth full of buttons and nuts, squirrely philosopher, around a mouth full of wuh, sorry, *weeds*, she winks her wax teeth at me. Her wheat tax. Eat lead, kid. That there's the writing on the wall.

Every night the sun shows its negative side, it rolls over from China and sprays us with its lead gun and our heads just melt. I say, no, it's not China, baby, it's America, and then we both take a belt. We belt up our mouths. We mute it for different seasons.

Then we leg it over to the corner to chew on cords. We go over.

We go over like a lead balloon. Like a baleen in the punched-out mouth of a whale. Like one ounce of plastic in a healthy albatross's gut, two ounces equals a dead albatross. Which is why

I'm under the pinchcrib looking for a sock.

I'm under the sock-muck looking for a mug. I'm looking for a warm-up and a pick-me and a -tune. To pick the lock of a sleeping baby wearing its millstone of candy around its neck. Noone can slip nothing past me and my baby.

Or pull one over on us.

Or push us over.

Not noone can.

3. In which my kid proves a hero of the injection. Next stop a wrestly Mercury-mask, stops up the ears, stops up the nose, swims in the blood, sews painful wings onto those baby ankles, but they'll thank you for it. My kid's got her own pod of roll-up dolphins in her spangly blood, swimming and sieving in her alien scenes.

After the check-up, I see the doctor in the parking lot. Can she recognize my kid without her chart? I want desperately for my kid's face to be recognizable; I wouldn't recognize it myself if it weren't tied on. I try to draw the doctor's attention to us. I ring the stroller 'round my car. My kid's dingle tires sink deeper into the tar.

4. In which the tar is mud. *Girasol tamales*, Parish of St. Bavo, Women, Infant and Children's clinics all stipple-cell all sinking into the mud. No such lug today. Burning bright. Which makes the tar for melting. Which makes a Melchior.

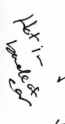

Alchemist's bauble or philosopher's stone stowed on the shelf amid the unused Pampers and summer togs. Salamandrine, my kid

is burning in the back seat. Shit.

5. For my kid, I'm reorganizing songs by degree of scratchiness. Pod of whales in the developer bath: check. Voice of the buried ear-strumpet: check check. How she scratched at the earth from where she was buried. How she scratched at the box to come out.

It can only come through in negative, the math which is take-away, so feel it out. We're two bats short of a deck. Two bats. A nighttime visit to Pere Lachaise, a lifetime visit to Salome this veil of shadows, on the verso, hat-trick, hat-check, headless, consciousness, you have boot up to port into it, please, boot up. I'm going to wrap you and then wrap you again and then the spirit will rap you and then you can throw up.

Throw out the grave digger's song. Soil and response.

The arc with which it falls into the grass all around. The crass grass which clasps us all to its seedy boosum,

sang the seedy vegan, the scribal eunuch bending at his song. Oh, enough obscene adam's apple. Obscene 'adam's

choice'. Raunchy early Modernistic occultist, I've got a
child, here, varmit. Ghost up!

6. In the cactile forest, my kid and I slouch the shadows.
Bale the fence. Cut the current. Fray the forest. Barb the
wire. Come on in. Long horns shift in the moonlight, it's
like a sea in your head for you to wrastle in. It's like a tire
burns. I wave her low. I wave her eyes closed. We look
through cattle eyes, smoke through our noses, tags in our
hairy ears. Our shoulders shift in ridges. Then we're up
on the ridge, we hunch through the eyes of six deputy-
lawmen. We've got us in our sights. Then we close like
the iron in the red in the ridge.

Slink out of sight like a species

salamander

you're paid to change

now change.

7. I need to buy socks but which socks? What can the kid
not kick off? And why won't the kid sleep? I ask the mirror. It's certainly nighttime you can tell just by looking in
the mirror, the way it slumps and tries to shie away. The
mirror is cracked from too many launchings and each
launch is a foothold where my kid can lodge or sag but

instead she's fitful, insists on jerking in time to the jumps she makes in the quarter. *In the quarter, in the quarter, just jitter and skitter on down. Catch a knife when it's falling, drive the spittle into the ground. Find me a fateful woman if you can. Find me a fateful woman if you can.* I'm clocked in junk, it's a racket, it keeps the kid awake, I have to hack it, I have to hack it up. I have to empty out the junkdrawer of the grave.

In the quarter, in the quarter, in the nickel in the dime, in the cash drawer, honey, that's where you find a real good time. Draw the ewer full of water draw the sewer full of lime, won't you stay the same forever, won't you ford that never twice.

My kid's alive a live live wire like Lethe the nevermore. Skinny kid, for a baby, everybody says. How she jumps right out the window through the eye of the needle and into the eye of the grave.

8. The doctor says if the kid won't start gaining soon we're going to have to take measures. Since we measure her constantly I say like what. The doctor is half-coralled, half-wild, skinny in the face. She turns her back to me to write in a chart. Her little stool shrieks as she turns around. It's freezing in here. That's what my kid says to the sock it's shoved in its mouth.

~ 50 ~

I'm in love with the doctor.

You should pay more attention to that kid.

9. Who has the money for that? We're on a launch split-ting over the sand. The wind touches everything, it's making an anthology. The sand is making a blessing. It flies up to smack the launch out of the air. It's a better parent than the launch. It cares about my kid, really cares. It sticks to all the bits and places in her plan.

As we clamber off the launch, the wind can't resist, can't let it rest, licks its blade and rifles my kid's breathweight hair. My kid's eyes split and tear. The ocean is feeling compulsive, whack whack whacking its head against the sand. My kid rocks on mini-knees, takes a step step then lifts its feet when it wants to get closer. Knocks itself down. Cuts feet face hands on the sand. Silica and rot-wort, rotwort and slime-bladder.

Some girls make lists. Poets and witches. And botanists, botanists.

I scoop up my kid and go island maiden, swaying my hipswitch all over the sand. My kid turns and turns and makes a turbine I let her drill into the sand.

The drill needs water to keep it from smoking.

Water comes out to fill the hole the drill bites with its bit.

Polyps for polyps. Fishbone eyes. Knucklebone corset. The whole corpse. The whole corpus. Like a porpoise, but with a purpose. Anima o' mine.

I gather up my kid. We're on a cigarette boat. We're on the moon which is the mom of the ocean.

The ocean, dumb like a kid.

The ocean is over and we didn't even get a chance to fire our guns.

I forgot, we're vipers. I forgot, we're snipers. I forgot, we're on a big-breasted schooner which is also known as Death-in-Life.

Now we're getting somewhere.

10. I have a minute to myself because my kid is sleeping. I leave the house. I stand in the driveway. The house is not a house but one end of a condo unit that hangs out on stilts over a useless hill. The decks were built by teenage meth addicts on a Christian recovery plan. Close-eyed

youth. Chain smoking. Our end juts up asymmetrically in a way that is impossible to photograph. You have to look at it. I am. I am standing in the driveway. I have been away from my kid for six minutes. Now I am standing in the cul-de-sac. A praying mantis is actually also here at my feet, and it does bend over itself like a mildmannered classical music deejay. I get in my car and listen to a mild-mannered classical music deejay who can barely bring himself to emit. I let the engine run, which eats up the air and makes it bad in the future for my kid.

Then I go put black roses on the graves at Pere Lachaise. You can get them at Kroger, and the leaves are red. It takes petroleum, but you have to do your homework, as the girl standing on the back of the bike said to the pedaling boy when they got just nudged by a bumper. You have to put in some effort. As they flew into the air like a roll of quarters or a wheel of fortune or any kind of wheel. I go put black roses on the graves. Then while my lipstick is burning off my face I drink a diet coke and my teeth smoke and then I go back to my kid. It's hot in her room and smells like diapers. I put her in her sundress, but then, when I take her outside, it's cold. Her shoulders are cold. I'm hoping we'll find her red shoe before her grandmother arrives. That would be my mother. We should take the axe when we go on walks like this, with our lips on.

VAMPIRES

11. My kid and I are vampires which means we're not supposed to get any sun. Her father is not related to us so he's not a vampire. I'm explaining this to the nurse who asks for our insurance card. Has any of your information changed. Yes I remembered we're vampires. She takes my card and scans it. The scanner won't take the image. The reason is obvious—we have no souls to photograph. We leave them at home when we have to go out in the day.

There are cemetaries in Mishawaka and the cemetaries are covered with the Chevys and Buicks of people driving across the grass to get to their fathers' graves. Everyone keeps the graves real nice and hardly lets the little flags bleach out or the little black roses you can get at Kroger when you're checking out. There is not much for my kid and I to do at these cemetaries except sit in the exhaust fumes and get hot in our black clothing. Black baby clothing: you can find it.

12. Your kid is not gaining weight what do you feed her. Applesauce. Ivory. Buttons. Shoerubber. Newsprint. A toy dog.

That sounds fine that should be working but she's not gaining. I'm going to ask you to keep this diary for a week. We'll send a technician from our home health team to review your diary. If we can't find a practical solution we're going to have to begin a rather expensive round of tests.

I have to look at round things to catch what the doctor says. They have to collect. Stethoscope mouth, diploma seals, safety whirlwind, plastic cup, the stool she has to sit on to write up her reports, it must be mandated, stool only, big lolling wheels, my kid's eyes with their schools inside and all the pupils shrinking in the light.

13. Thomas Hardy I'm thinking of selling my kid but not my wife on the Internet. Not my wife because I don't have my wife on hand she left me, and by my wife I mean myself, and by my husband, my kid's father, who is always pretending not to be a vampire, through no fault of his own, someone has to pay the bills and sleep at night and purchase the allnight Internet service. I'm thinking of selling my kid for some grog, because my kid is getting in the way of my destiny. Is it gruel or grog? Without my kid I have a better chance of becoming the mayor of casterbridge, and of grog, and of my destiny.

Seriously. When I look at my kid it's like my flesh falling off my face it's like aging many granite centuries it's like being in sunlight. The gentle, corrosive enchantment on my skin.

14. My kid and I are trying harder. I'm setting the example, here. We consume a field of corn. It's gold and burns the throat, all husks and sepulchres. When we see a harvester we duck into our car. The harvester burns by,

of course like a harbinger, and like a harviture, indesti-
tude, what's that. It's strong and paltry because defined,
it moves its mass up and down the gridded field, the field
is in fibrous layers like muscle but made of a husky matter, the combine's bustle must burn to the touch but who
could touch it but the huge exhaustive grainy investiture
it tugs behind it like a shower of gold. Like a randy god
that got too close got its toe caught in the mechanicals.

I got my eye caught in the mangle. I'm seeing mash-eyed.
My kid is squinnying thru the marrow in the pork chop
on the wide dull luck of the plate. The tabletop pretends
to be wood for awhile. Font of life. It's wide as a wind-
shield, greased with love. We swallow a lot of bullshit
about small towns, co-ops, steely cylinders of feed, pie,
flags, groaning semis, a lot of bullshit about coffee, three-
wheelers, quarters, American breakfast, trailers, hard-
tops, hair salons, a lot of peepshow about a motel. No
semis here except bobtails. The fencerails and highwires
are thick with bobtails, they perch their horseless ca-
booses in system-busting polygagging flocks.

American owned. Family operated.

15. Owe owe owe owe owe we owe owe we owe owe owe
owe we owe wowed

Owe owe owe owe owe we owe owe we owe wowed.

Owened. Speedthrift. Windered, spedthru, spider wow.

Owed and wowed. Owed and wounded. Owned and windowed. Owed and wow. Wondrous wow. Wondrous eyed. Wondrous forehead.

Owed and owed, owed and opened

Fabled, vapored. Walking woman wove an oval novel vow.

Vowelled

O be wed.

O be done it.

Down and dusted.

Ode and wowed.

Ode and wowed and wounded. Oven-saw, that everyone has heard.

Sewed a windburn everyone has wowed.

Severed an ode owned ode crowed inlet winded crowd and wow.

Wined and dinedn't, didn't

owe woe, didn't debit

didn't credit didn't wow

didn't winded

didn't ow-ow didn't wow

didn't voodoo didn't double

didn't woah-woah didn't wow

didn't dixit didn't vincit didn't vow

then and now

the toe-hold is a lariat

loosed a loose noose over now

posse

Robert Frost?

Kara Walker.

16. At Tar-mart, I buy my kid a pink hooded bone shirt. Now she looks like a fossil. Her bones glow green in the dark of the tar. Dressed as a deodorized death, my kid can ooze through the ozoneless truckwash like any other child bride. *I have a rendezvous with destiny.* Noone can stop it. Noone can know it's Death-in-life, also known as waking-death, also known as potential, pessimistic, also failure-to-thrive. My little pony draws death by the noose, by the nose, she likes to grab my nose or pull my lazy hair while she's nursing which waters my eyes and makes my crazy come out. But it brings death to noone, except me. Mine, the bit my kid holds in its mouth. ✓

The councilman from Florida talks to the virtual mother about her virtual five year old Q. But what should I tell my daughter A. Tell her you found her a sweet boyfriend who will bring her presents. Virtual but not virtuous, non-present, bring her presence, bring her a decoy posed as a mother the five-year-old posed as nowhere splayed out in the lap of the eye of the councilman's mind in snapshots of nowhere flat squares without vanishing points and it's nowhere that's so frightening the blank nowhere in their eyes.

My kid and I have rituals to decoy time we have a chalice, a red cloth and a deck of cards. A taroc pack. I deal from the top. The little hand switches. The little doll barrel rolls with a spear in its gut, hiccupping, bubbles. The big hand rotates grave. The cat comes back: I sing to my kid while trying to recall the sign language from resuscitation class. Of our future, the cards say this: a gas album, an albatross, a big ice floe, a dancing double bear. A cloud furrows and grave inches closer. Make that a drowning bear, fear death by warming. The table shifts its legs restively, the pharmacy-themed bar hovers into view, opens its magazine, grins its staple teeth, its caplets, its buttons, only say the word and I'll no longer be a capulet, a children's chewable, an art-n-choke.

Ask the dead of the plot: how many square inches? I wave my hand over a trove of blocks, a plaything, a conceit. A wraith materializes. Come closer. Answer me.

STAMPS

17. My kid just materialized ten minutes ago. Ten seconds. Half a life. A half-life. A minuet. I'm doing the mathwork on the back of the form. We need to go on stamps. We need to fill out the fugal, slotted paper. My husband is working the graveyard shift—naturally. Religion? Blood type? I'd lost hope but now it's only a matter of time before he's a convert to our way of non-life.

At the farmer's market, the working poor and the working poor face off over piles of sustenance. The working poor points at a potato, and the working poor says 'dollar a bucket.' The working poor picks out four peppers and the working poor shakes out a sack. Two bucks. The sustenance piles in different molecular arrangements, here adding up to a head of cabbage, and here of head cheese. Jalepeños not covered by stamps. Eggrolls not covered by stamps. One dozen, three bucks. The kids in tight orbitals are perambulated. Fifty cents. The crowd pushes by (like death-in-life, slim channels, alley of stalls), there are puppies ticking, little things have faster heartrates, no charge, everyone says to my kid hey bright eyes, he don't miss a thing now does he. It's a little girl, I say, deflating the exchange. The flow drags us along for awhile. My kid woofs at the pumpkins.

My kid and I are out of line out of whack out of order off the plot off the reservation in closed talks in tandem in negotiations in a thrilling starstudded race against time in which we play the stars and time plays the entire circumference of circumstantial evidence. We make waste and we make our case. The paper piles up around us, as do the guest stars.

18. My kid has blue eyes, I don't know why, although my husband has blue eyes, that's not a reason. That's not an argument. This cold we're passing back and forth ropes in my husband and now we all flop together in the Kiddie Corral like a bunch of half-dead cowboys without cows,

~ 61 ~

without boys, without ropes, without hats, without songs, without nothin but a demonstrable exhaustedness which flattens us like a herd of hooves. My kid demonstrates the barrel roll and gets a rug burn. I demonstrate the torpedo roll but my kid won't try it; it can be wimpy like that. I demonstrate salmon, flying skate, I display on ice with my fat eye clear and non-wandering. I once was lost but now I'm found and now I'm for sale by the ounce and the pound. I'm slender, spender, so it's gloves-off while supplies last. Offer not good in conjunction with other offers and void where prohibitive by law. In the case of two, the lesser value applies.

I'm not bought. I tick nervously.

The home nurse sits on a couch sipping the diet coke I brought her. I ask her how is it and she tells me good. But why do you think your baby stopped gaining weight. The tests came back fine, she should be fine. In reply I wave my hand vaguely. Everything in this time zone enters and stagnates, turns over, is used and used up. The milk rots in my nose. The meat gels on the plate. The vegetables stain and corrode. I show her the refrigerator and it's all there, cold, all the food you could want, in place and corroding. The problem is it's not blood. The problem is all available blood comes from animals, even human animals, and that disgusts me. My kid and I need synthetic blood. Machine blood. I heard they have that for soldiers. Is it true? I ask the nurse. Now I recall that maple syrup circulates nutrients in the tree which makes it a kind of blood. Is syrup blood? I ask the nurse.

19. My kid has six teeth. The first two were a fine, razory pair but now she hosts a clunky array like family portraits smuggled out of the closed empire in the darned skirt of her mouth.

I give her stakes to chew, steaks, a bracelet, a bracelet of hair around the bone, a relic, the loose skin of my arm, my gaze, an epithelial reliquary where variety-of-experience used to lodge.

Night is swollen at the gum but pain makes the day grain through and accumulate in a frieze of severalness and stacked sufficiency. I strap my kid to my back and we strike our gaze into windshields and chrome detailing. The faces of flowers, the grate of a flag, the airplane's loud belly, any hide with a face. We jump out into day clock-clad and waving our moveable parts.

We bury our gaze there like a bone.

20. The compound arrives. The home nurse brings the first month's dose in her hatchback, packed with pamphlets

~ 63 ~

and poorly photocopied checklists I can barely make out. I can barely make it. I can dose my kid with a bottle or a port will be implanted in its gut. I have to fill out more forms to pay for next month's and the forms crowd around me like an infection like an infarction like an epithelial farce.

21. Nightwatch in the cemetery. A searching, a scratching which is a crosshatching. The engraving comes into view.

Dead stratified squamous, keratinized epithelial cells.

Even at night, we move around inside the dead parts of ourselves.

My kid is asleep in her carseat in a nest of sweatshirts. The moon is a hopeful zero in a nest of debt.

In my kid and in myself, mucous membranes are lining the inside of the mouth, the esophagus, and part of the rectum. Other, open-to-outside body cavities are lined by simple squamous or columnar epithelial cells.

A gust comes through the cemetery and it's an idea, I can stand on knifepoint on the edge of it.

My shoes are off so I can feel my bones through the cold. Stasis, metastasis, tap tap tap. If the soles of my feet are pierced then nutrition will run into the grass. I jump back. The idea is nixed, then razed. Vines lock my wrists to the car.

The insides of the lungs, the gastrointestinal tract, the reproductive and urinary tracts, the exocrine and endocrine glands. The outer surface of the cornea are all lined with such cells.

Without ideas I call to my familiars:

Secretion, absorption, protection, transcellular transport, sensation detection, and selective permeability.
I wrest my wrists away from the livid plants and climb back into the car. Through the gunmetal doors, through the wind-braced windows, I snake the pedestal locks. Again I'm with my kid.

Endothelium (the inner lining of blood vessels, the heart, and lymphatic vessels) is a specialized form of epithelium. Another type, mesothelium, forms the walls of the pericardium, pleurae, and peritoneum.

You connective tissue. You nervous tissue. You're fine by me. Fly by.

22. It's Halloween. I shove my kid into a dusk costume her uncle sent. I shove her into the car. Families are mustering in front of the town hall, its duct-shaped parking

lot with a little numb flagpole ticking up across from the Wendys, the Arbys, the Burger King and the Taco World. It's five o'clock, seventy degrees. The traffic in the drivethrus is thick, digests wraiths and witches through lanes marked out with plastic guidelines and plastic characters fitted with speakers. Thank you for your order please drive around.

The mayor will hand out candy, but for now he's caught in the peristalsis outside Wendys. He waves to the crowd from the cab of his stuck truck.

It's five o'clock and a rank of men descends from the shelter with pillowsacks in hand, only under and overdressed for the weather, in workshirts or sports-team cerements, with the raked-gaits of their former professions, artists and workmen and accountants, their bones and wrecked joints remembering. They mount bikes in a decomposed phalanx or stalk on in their buttoned-on fat, their hair shorn or furled stiff as conquistadors' helmets, as upraised pikes and scythes, they course against traffic with their fused-socket gazes held high above our heads. They pass by with the purposefulness of the dead

and glint off down the road like a ghost army.

The mayor is extruded from Wendys, crosses traffic, the kids surround the smoking face of his truck which could part and birth a giant burger from its hood but doesn't.

Someone puts candy in my kid's hand and it chews the purple wrapper rapturously, dropping the melting chocolate buds onto the street.

I tug my kid out of the duck costume in the backseat of the car and cruise home with the windows down so dark can come inside. So dark can cool it

tenderly,
black like me.

23. Back at the complex, the kids ring the bell, scrape their carpals against the emptying belly of the plastic bowl where I've dumped damp sticks of gum.

Be safe! I hear wringing from the other doorsteps. Be safe! I chime.

My kid's lying on the carpet in a wet diaper, coughing at a cartoon dad to get his attention. Be safe!

Then it's real night and the bell is silent, the streets are silent. My husband is home and folded up in sleep, his work van parked outside like a plot device, one of those vans with the ladder on the side.

When the bell picks up again it wakes up Salamandrine. I don't answer the door. An egg breaks on the window, nutritiously. The weathermap frays the tv. The counties jump all over each other. Then it suddenly clears and we watch some innings, unzipped by the storm, the legs of the umpire walking around with the head of the slugger over its head. Salamandrine claps her hands and the heads jump bodies, run bases headless, animated by the game.

When the sirens pick up we sit in the basement. We still have power but hold our flashlights anyway. The sound rolls over to one side, the light snuffs out and the storm heaves by.

Out in the morning light, garbage, paper bones, broken pumpkins, shattered sugar litters the streets. The mailbox is passed out in the gutter. Neighbors eat breakfast behind the broken windows, peering out as if the world were on tv. Egg yolks plaster leaves to the van. My husband hoses it down with a flood of curses. The ladder smiles like a punched out street.

The nurse is needed at the hospital and cancels her visit.

24. Salamandrine is growing!

Tumor Flats

I live in Tumor Flats, formerly known as Taco Flats for the high percentage of Latins, even more formerly Elite Tacos, now also known as The Waste Land. If you want to know how I came this low, look around, kid, everybody's falling. I was never what you call a straight arrow but I made my way, Mercury Shoals, Muscle Flats, where I cut a record in the shower of a trailer. I wore a standup collar, fake hair, I had a velvet repel, I was shooting up life by the spoonful, but then my grind grew a rind that grew bitter and bitterer till my gears just went rust. Now I'm practically incarcerated in my recliner, glimming the smear world through a rip in my sack. But through this nick in my glass I spy the bright world, the little kids heavy with knowledge, their necks stalked, they need a constant tumor tutor to hold their throats open, check the lines that change their fluids, run their chemical baths.

But that's the bright world: palliative care, case histories, file o' facts. Here in Tumor Flats you got your types. There's the occasional cute girl, though they seem to disappear at 12 and reappear at 40. There's a harmless klepto, a celebrity. She moves amid the tumors, taking useless metal you can't even sell: the zipper off a fetid coat, the last husk of moonshine in a cleaned-out Coke. She wears a caramel flip teased high at the crown and a claret gown cut up past the thigh, she wears slippers, she used to sing in a variety show, the money-colored curtains used to part and part for her, I remember, inside the little votive box that flickered like a penny candle, and the violins screeched high at her entrance like fat like the streaks in her hair.

There is a tourist today amid the tumors. Spreading rumors, which are tumor cash, deprivation currency, degradation debit card, a fat lip federal face. Fat the rumors and thin the fate. There is a philatelist who's come in for a lick. Let him have it. There's a slumming fatalist, but she won't last a day among these tumors. There's a butch fatale who is an optimist. There's an entire olive-clad decrepit army called the Army of Life. There's a femme arabesque in the sky above the denaturing plant. They've laid off all the workers like spoiled eggs but the plant just goes on making cool whip from its own innards like a concrete goose. In the yard there's a lot of muck that won't burn, we tried it. In any case the air today is an outside story about an inside deal, a high-inside pitch, a false-bottomed truck, a suitcase not for the faint of heart. All is sugar and spit. Then all is drone. It's partly my fault. I can't hear properly, can't make the transmission. The top part of my audibles just split like a sack of sugar, then the lower part like an ass of slacks, so I only had the middle, but I got no truck with the middle. My father had a truck garden and my mother sold eggs. That was how they got through the last dip of this merrie-go-round. Then these horses got hit with the virus and froze with that whacked-out mask of fear for a face.

How I Lost My Hearing, Ending Up in Tumor Flats:

The End.

A gunshot I hear again and again. My sleep of noisesome ricochet. But my days are so plush and thick, bathed in a fluid that doesn't care how it got started, and I never hear anything sneaking up on me, but somehow feel it and look up, like today I look up through the plastic, and I see the klepto smiling at me, and her smile is dazzling, it has black inside, and black plastic covers both her eyes, but sunlight smiles in her stiff hair, and her skin is somehow rosy like a gift where her red gown parts, and I offer her my broken watch, full of metal, and she won't take it, but when I leave it on a sill she swipes it when we're both not looking, and then she's gone, and she beams munificent, after all, she bears riches, and she takes the haze with her from door to door as she tries to strip them of their bad luck charms.

The Army of Life might be a problem. They're soldiers from way back, believe in order in some vague oppressed way, and they're still wearing the clothes they got discharged in. No matter how many lines they did, doses they shot, scams they ran, cars they fenced, mamas they robbed, kids they beat, shit jobs they held and lost, they think the sickness comes from everyone else in the world but them. 'It ain't right, it ain't right!' they like to whine, and then they march together in little handfuls of three or five or whatever they can muster, whoever is awake and angry and not in his tumor sleeping one off. Sometimes they form a kind of citizen's brigade and hassle the klepto, because she's out in plain sight, they try to get a hand in her gown and see what she's got there. When I see that I toss a few bottles at them and they wheel like whining dogs. Then they say to me, "Slick, you ain't law-abiding if you help that whore." I pretend I can't hear them, zip myself back into my wall.

There's some fires a few nights, and on the third night someone lights up the plastic tarp that's wrapped around my tumor, and its fumes make the walls flex and smart, but then it goes out, they must not have wanted to waste moonshine to get the fire going right. In the morning I inspect the damage: the burnt plastic has warped and then cooled in knots and shards, making for my tumor a weird and brittle shell, spiky and aggressive as a thorny crown.

But just when I'm starting to worry about the Army of Life, some cat in a suit shows up with a clipboard and fifty U.S. dollars stamped on a debit card for each patriotic sum' bitch and marches them all off from Tumor Flats, what a sad little pack of rats they make, each wearing an orange intake bracelet and marching in a greasy, haggard line.

Then it's quiet for the rest of the day. I'm not friendly with anyone to ask what's going on, except the klepto, she goes everywhere and sees everything but she doesn't talk, just goes on beaming that Jackie-O-smile like an energy source, that's Jackie-O not Jackie-K, Jackie-O, gliding through her many mansions like a single continuous tomb, more ageless than in her brittle youth, more relaxed now that she's seen the worst that Jackie-K was always bracing herself for. And let's not talk about Jackie-B, French class queen. The klepto sits with me late afternoon when the sunlight settles into the greasy toxin that gilds the air like sticky pollen, and the scraps in her lap also catch the light, and we watch the tumors revamp and reformat themselves, some casting an iridescence, others growing hair or teeth or pissing an acrid metallic stream, mine bulging with a springy mass that cracks the shell to sharp pieces that dig into its slick flesh until it expands again, grows an epithelium that sheathes the plastic.

✷ I won't deny it: I've got a thing for the klepto. It's the way she moves as if she has shocks and struts: the way she glides like she's on whitewalls. It's the way her belted gown draws a line at her absolute center: saw here to cut the lady in half. Her sunglasses make a stage of every outing, and she steals from us like it's charity work, divine intervention. One night I drink a lick of moonshine—it only takes a lick in my condition to thin out my vision— till I see straight through the Flats to her tumor, which is dermoid, lined with teeth, they're slick as car keys, and I see her in her one movie role, the flop with cops that used to run on late-night, how she fought with the killer as the klieg lights blew their shadows up three stories tall on the wall behind them, above a mob that was looking the other way, at New Jersey.

One day I greet her with a movie line:

Sweetheart, it's time to prove you're good for more than filling out that tight court stenographer's get-up.

And then, because she doesn't answer, I say her line, too:

Bud, I know I can be a good cop and I'm ready to prove it.
I just need my chance. Just give me my chance.

She smiles at me like all the headlights at the drive in,
turned on me, and then she stops and fits her lips over
her teeth.

Then I just want to so I lead her into my tumor and fold
back her gown, work off her shell-colored panties.

Then I don't see her for awhile, and then I see her again,
she's standing at my fence with her arms hanging over
into my yard, and she's got a bunch of orange intake
bracelets hanging off each wrist. Up close I can see they're
still printed with serial numbers in a grey print that's
wearing off. The orange is also cracking off the Tyvek. I
kiss her neck which smells like powder. Then I follow her
like a camera man down the allée between tumors.

And as I follow her form like a flaw in the film, a
bleedthrough from another scene, then I'm elsewhere,
I'm following a stiff lilac skirt, high pony tail and rounded white church collar down a hallway that can't be more
than ten feet, but takes a sinner's forever as the hot dark
air thickens, deep in the house, and pushes back against

what we want to do. On the bedsidetable there's a Bible open and a place claimed with a ribbon so red I can't help but put a finger to it as Treesa stands in front of me and starts to lift up that good girl skirt like a miracle. Yea, like a mountain being lifted away.

Amen, saints! Amen, saints! The radio casts a call for witness as I keep one thumb on the hammer and one eye on the cashier and one eye squinted, though Treesa's brother told me time and again to keep both eyes open, fool, keep both eyes open. And god bless the doctors may they be as sharp as they can possibly be but all healing comes from Jesus Lord I know you know that I said all healing comes from Him, Saints!

But that weren't the bullet that took my hearing away and added it to one long reverberating crash that my brain can make in my dreams but another bullet when Treesa was with me in the showerbath where earlier we had made the record and now with everyone drunk in the front room she was here with me again it was a room with but one high flat window and when Treesa sprung away from me one bullet caught her in the belly and another one burnt the lobe of my ear as it exploded into the wall.

And now I stand with the klepto before a little grassy decline and heaped at the bottom is about two-thirds of the Army of Life mostly lying on their sides like hieroglyphics with hospital gowns licking away from their old man limbs instead of their discharge jackets.

Their own flesh shrinks away from them like it did in life, but no more than it did in life, their hair has been shaved short so their skulls show, and some of them have a shunt or a button behind their exposed ears, and their faces are a suffocated purple and their lips are black. They don't smell; it's as if they've been freeze dried.

Up the other side of the decline is a wall of wire diamonds turned on their axes and beyond that is the strait and beyond that is the bright world where a low chalk white building first smiles then goes blank. In this light its doors and its windows are a plasma blonde and something glints on top like tinsel, probably concertina wire gracing the epithelium of the roof.

It's a damn bad scene, in the middle of the afternoon, the klepto in her sweltering red robe and honey wig, the Army all lined up like the worst thing you know about yourself, repeated again and again, pinned in place, their black lips peeled back from their vicious teeth. I trade some of what I have for a bucket of moonshine, burn up the bodies that night. A chemical smell flies up like a curtain that goes up and up and into the Heaven, always rising for the scene that never starts. I stand and watch that smell rush up. When I turn around the rushing's in my ears and the smell settles on the tumors in a light blue powder that is quickly absorbed, causing some to go parched and split, others to swell and gloss.

I carry the rushing and the smell to my own tumor and lie down in my box of rags. The next day I don't feel so good, I feel bad. I've got a cloudy jug of water and a glass with desert colored vinyl strips on its exterior. I fill the glass to the third stripe and drink it down to the first. I try to do this as slowly as I can, to spare the water and my stomach, which is smarting and bucking today like a melted motherboard. My skin is fried in the thin places, friable, and there's a acridness between my eyelids and my eyes. My tumor is kitted out with plastic grills which house a vent that doesn't work anymore but I stare at the grills anyway trying to pull the air with my eyes through the slots.

A couple of days later I guess I pull myself onto my recliner where I can see out into the lanes. I see the glinting eye of the clipboard again, the blue and white suit of the man holding it, his stack of debit cards thick in the clamp. This time the fee is twenty-five dollars a head, and despite the cut price and although word must have spread about the pit burial of the Army of Life, the line is somehow longer this time, composed of sallow, thin, or unnaturally swollen bodies. Their skin has no natural luster, and the sun behind them lights up not the red blood in their veins but a straw colored viscous matter that stands like ill will in their limbs and couldn't circulate worth nothing.

It's like a clearance sale; the desire of people to buy the stuff rises with the sinking prices. Except here what they're buying is their own death. Their own long visit to the pit. Even the earth won't cover them up. Even the ground won't have them.

As if to respond to my thoughts, one middle-aged lady in a huge faded vacation tee-shirt turns to me with eyes that say, But sweetie, my death won't make me anything if I wait for it right here, now will it.

And then she's replaced in the hasp of my vision by the klepto, who smiles a wide smile and waits in the line with her hands clasped before her like she's walking for the communion rail.

Now she's taking a shuffle forward, and then a shuffle, till she's at the head of the line, refusing a proffered debit card and a bracelet and reaching instead for the clipboard, the ballpoint pen in the man's hand. The startled man and the klepto push their arms back and forth a few times like dancing, the clipboard pressed upright between them, until he comes to his senses and flings her to the side. She lands on her hands and knees, her dress back and her ass exposed. For a few moments she's like an heiress groping for diamonds in the dust. He's patting all his pockets and the front of his coat until he finds another pen and continues with the next person. As a goon gets the klepto upright and leads her off to a dusty shuttle she waves right at me like she can see inside this tissue to where I'm watching. I'm watching. The flash of the pen in her hand.

CHARISMA

1. Morning goes on adjusting the circus-colored umbrella till it shades my pale daughter, asleep on a dune. Up in the town, my lover slams his tumbler down onto the checkerboard spread, the bare dreg of spirit jumping like a flirty girl. He sketches the rump of a horse on the bill.

I remember when she was born: crocus-colored. Billiard gold. Then under the lamp, she developed.

The horse wears the chain of a mayor. Fatuosities in three languages spring from its rump.

The fringed shawl bites my ankles, the glare adjusts. The dull sea shifts like a restless sleeper. Goes over to the other side.

2. Let's pass the time, let's play a game.
What did all good girls bring on the train?
Good girls who love their daddies. *Patria*.

 A my name is Alice and I brought ammunition. B my name is Berthe and I brought bandages. C my name is Claudette and I brought cyanide. D my name is Denise and I brought dynamite. E my name is Esther and I brought ether. F my name is Frances and I brought fuses, flannel, fingerless gloves for the mountains at night. G my name is Genie and I brought grease. H my name is Hilde and I brought hatchets. I my name is Inez and I brought ink.

3. We were in the blue apartment when the news struck. A yellow banner, the color of thick levee water or organ failure or a failure of nerve lashed the base of the screen. I was entertaining my lover, my feet laced into the red ballet shoes he loves so well. We carried on. My daughter was with the woman who serves as grandmother to all the motherless children of the tenement, and when we finished I fished her out from a sea of urchins. She turned her teeth to me. Guiding her up the steps, I said, *we're going on the journey, my little mark, my little minx. You've got to stand on the case to make it close.*

This town is shelved on a promontory. Beyond here there's nothing but water, folded and refolded like an intimate silk that cannot be replaced or cleaned. Precious, precious salt sea, seed of pearls. I try to make it lie flat, it catches and snags. I am looking into the round mirror for the trace of age. My boldest smile pulls the wrinkles flat.

4. In the first hours of the calamity stills of the bright, shredded crowd cycled by on screens, pain running out of the center like a bloodshot eye. Her body could not be seen. It had evacuated even the hole cut out for her in the roof of the gleaming black vehicle, where the blow-up slammed her skull against the frame. Space and time rutted in a vanishing point, a network of stops and losses frayed out from that moment. From which point everything has happened, to which drain everything has run.

I readied myself and my daughter for the journey, all the while prattling to my lover to keep him from going out into the street. Even a quick errand could have been fatal—not to him, but to me. A turned head, and my daughter and I would have been lost. I've faced crises like that before, so I knew what to talk about to keep him: his rivals, sexual and professional, a ribbon of talk which tied him to his chair. Meanwhile I pulled out the old suitcase and packed it with necessities: negligees, dressing gowns, slips, a shift, all the filmy materials necessary for keeping quarters with a man, as well as atomizers, powders, lockets, fans, scarves, handmirrors, and finally the child's own stockings, blouse, nightgown and brush. I handed her her coffin clothes, buttoned her black coat. She tugged on her high-button boots, then kept dolefully to a corner as I dressed myself, pulling my curls down below a chic blue hat. Finally I lifted her standing onto the shut case. Her small boots with their polished toes aligned perfectly between the two striped bands. I hooked her fingers with mine and swung them as the lock clicked shut.

5. J my name is Jouer. K my name's Kalumny. L my name
is Lassitude. M my name is Hunger. N my name is Nihil.
O my name is Oh of course

[handwritten annotations:]

French "to play" →

Calumny → misrepresentation to harm someone's reputation

fired

the absence of anything / nothing ↓

hotel

6. Of course we're the only guests. The eggpink furnishings have gone grey, greasy dust silted through to the bones of the armchair, clotting the grain in the wood, the filigree in the lampglass. He leaves immediately and we unpack, then go out ourselves, walking a gravel road to the interior. Stucco houses like outworn summer shirts. My ears fill with a humming, a machine sound from childhood. I sleep in my mother's bed while she sews for hours, hems and seams, the fabric piled on one chair and pulled smooth on another Then she transfers me to the sheet-covered couch where I sleep through till morning. The machine in its olive vinyl jacket like my future baby daughter, waiting to be revived.

In the town rests a dusty millinery with a shelf of outmoded hats splayed like specimens. Birds'-wing helmets, zippered peaks dented artfully like bombarded ziggurats, the fur trim formerly gracing a rodent's spine now framing red LCDs, wiry newts and dipping antennae arrayed like a pliant adolescent crown. I buy the whole lot. Later, the milliner's son rides out to the hotel on his bicycle, hatboxes buoying him in every direction, a cardboard cloud clamped to the crossbar with his knee.

7. My daughter eats an omelet in the bar-café, while warships parade on the screen. They are exercising lamely in the strait like divorcees in a shipboard pool. Each raises a cannonade, each trails a modest train. The Pow'r is elsewhere. I butter a crust.

8. My lover, it transpires, will stay elsewhere, rooms over the bar-café where there's space for his work, his easel, his charcoal, his folders of soft salvaged paper and pots of noxious glue. At his work he's steadfast as a miner and I'm just as happy to be separate from the drudgery it entails. A maid may bring his milk and meat. He arrives at my rooms at odd and irregular hours; I make a palette for my daughter in the common parlor then join him upstairs. The arrangement suits me, though the possibility of abandonment lies like a lobe of dense fruit at the edge of this cold plate. It has its skin to me, covering flesh of uncertain age and quality underneath. At night when I'm sleepless I study its full curve, turn on the radio, music touches me as moonlight strokes the smooth tones of the beach. But rare is the night when I can't sleep.

9. On the dusty screen above the bar, the dead woman's son addresses the camera. His hair is a smart black wave, a helmet a knight would wear to battle Death. He's dressed in a white and yellow cricket sweater, he looks crisp and untouchable, but gothic arches over him like clasped and wringing hands.

And the sound of air filling all the holes in the microphone like wringing wringing hands.

The bartender reaches up and with a slap changes the image to a jewel-green field. Players tilt up and down the screen. Flag-wielding fires in the stands. *Olé, Olé*, the rechristened stadium. When I was a girl, that stadium was busy as a market, a market of specimens for slaughter filled the stalls. Oh, but the old times are gone—to where? Everywhere. *Olé, olé.*

The dead birds on my hat salute the beak-black, empty corners. The kind of beak that Death would wear.

Later I gather my shawl around my shoulders and do my Spanish dance, my silver watch slipping halfway down my forearm. It was a gift from my lover, but now I can't find him in the crowd.

Brava, olé.

Time stops

10. At this moment when forward motion stops completely, time is an echo of the train. A visual echo. Maybe something's wrong with the film. The train's stopped. Smoke curls around the train like a second dragon. Time's commuters peer at its flank. What city is this, what station? Move to the back of the luck, please, it chants over and over again, in Hindu and Marathi, and leave the station through gate number one. Move the train and leave the station. Smoke can collect itself, it can make its own way. But for now it stays. It circles itself like a dragon. It erases the train. It makes a cranial bell of the stuttered gables. It raises its stakes. Like a smoke-cure, to clear the hive, it rises, and like a bee-cure, to cleanse the brain, it shudders down. I heard it die, I herd its pain. Can I be the one to lie down now. Can I be the one to lie. I ate the gold knob and now the face is frozen. I ate the gold fob and now the chin's collapsed. Can I be the one who has hid my berries in a pail under the pile of luggage. Lungage. Incendiaries, I mean. Under the language. Move to the back and towards door number one. And exit the station. I came like a girl to the story, to the room where the bears were asleep. No. To the room from which the bears were missing. To the room without bears: Russianless remainders. No, threadbear. No, roulette. Full chambers. A thousand threads accounted for all. Then I was the one who spun gold of it, then I wove up and down the sheet. Intoxicated, on the median stripped. Then I was

the one wound up in it, then I was the one asleep. Then fate poured out three helpings, the little, the big, and the mean. For history rewords big eaters, reworks them. I stood up and ate the grain, it reworked what lay in my gut, and it was bitter coming up. Then I spoke whole cloth without mincing, I spoke bolts, and what I vomited was gold cloth: fate. Fake, fake, fake, fake blessings, greening the neck like fate. (Limber fate, where is thy jack) Cold, cold, cold, cold blessings, a slate beach makes a cradle makes a grave, the fish lies down in the barrow and wakes up perverted, preserved in its gravid scales, a saint. It stays perfect till it's eaten. But life is no saint. To be alive is to be corrupted. Make room. Make moon. At the back of the bank. In the box of the train. Next we'll showerbath in the gin from this fizzle, this flash of it, this flask of fate, we'll make a goo of it, we'll make a hash. Fate or bust. At the next stop, the next station.

11. Two dank days cast the entire town belowdecks, and then the sun blazes back to life unexpectedly and the whole town is out on the beach, black drapeaux against the ochre sand. My lover is here as well, having abandoned the bar-café, and I think the beach must sink and the town rise on its shelf when the population swarms this little strand. The priggish townsfolk now strew the beach like garbage, now litter the sea. I pin a chartreuse ribbon in my daughter's long curls so I can pick her out. I see my lover standing far out in the tide, thick as a boxing buoy, lifting and dropping his arms, squinting back at the shore.

The next day the sun burns even closer. My daughter and I stagger out into it in our black costumes, lugging our parasols like tightrope walkers, to find the half-buried fenceposts stapled with bright orange signs. Each sign is stenciled with a swart blot representing a toxic species and the human nerve it kills and makes over in its own image. Underneath the details of this probable demise are spelled out, along with notice that the beach is closed. The many-limbed creatures pinwheel from post to post, and there's something in the casually fatal swerve away of each burnt dendrite that I easily recognize. A masculine stroke.

That afternoon my daughter has a light fever. Light is cast from her hot cheeks. I pay the landlady to sit by her side with cool cloths and set off for town. By the time I arrive my clothes are quite wet with perspiration. It pools under my breasts, at the small of my back, my face is hot and slick, each little hair on my arm bears its bead. When I reach the bar-café, my lover is elsewhere so I roast in his little room for awhile. I wrench my shoulder forcing open the window and, searching around for a matchbox, I find other absences traced in dust, various illegible smudges, fingerprints, then a place where a key's been swiped away.

12. My lover wants me to pretend I don't know him, then he wants me to make demands. I comply. For me it's easy, it's only natural. It's what a mask means: I have faces to show him. So many surfaces.

13. There is another person in this town. He appears only in peripheries, crowd scenes, he surfaces and he melts away, into and out of halfdoors and blind alleys. Black eyed, a black birthmark, a pale wide spreading brow. When they were shooting the thief at midday— first, where could we shoot him, get blood on the wall, or on the dogswalk, or on the well. We chose the dogswalk. Then, as smoke quickly improvised a dissolving signature over us, he was first to step away. 'I am a thief' they wrote in borrowed charcoal, argued over the spelling, the tense.

14. Nobody has to tell the townspeople to live as if in wartime. They just resume. They remember how to be occupied, unoccupied. Everyone who was a parent now had a grandparent alive in that other time, a grandparent now with his brow beneath the apple tree, split by its root, and each green apple singing sourly on the bough waiting to drop into a plump hand and worm to life.

So voices fall and prices rise. Mine are both high.

I am an experienced negotiator of small and large towns alike. I steer my skiff smoothly in placid or choppy seas and am partial to my profile, my daughter towed behind me like a rudder or a raft. This noon it was not my cheek that bore the fat red slap, the flush of shame, it was not me stained but those matrons who split like whitecapped seas around me when I entered their marketplace, and it was not my market drained of goods and the splintery stalls empty except for poor meat and spoiled leaves. I carried my purse close, I made for the bar-café, and paid for champagne and whipped egg for the child, as fortifying a meal as was called for in these febrile times, and I ordered for myself a cocktail in a glass barely wider than my knuckle, the hue of my biteknuckle ring green as the poison inside.

And my eyebrows inked a downcasting chevron to signal the poison inside

15. He wants me to pose like a prison wall, like the wanted poster. Then the sign beneath the sign. The cinderblock shoved away to reveal the pixel-wide chip of air. Second story. He wants me like the signal that's agreed upon in advance. Where hope leaps forward, light as a flame of vindication and revenge. Next he strokes my cheeks with charcoal, tidelines my fingertips up the inside of each arm. They anchor past my armpits, by the glands where cancer lies, a purse and a secret tucked beneath each breast. My torso is a long tract, a history of uprising, a deluge, a détente, here the mountains shifted to let in the rebel band, here the razorgrass clasped the fugitive to its breast, and here it betrayed him to the searching spyglass. The blow from the fat ring, smarting, biteknuckle, a ring of kohl under each eye, seeing eye, a red drop inked on each cheek, pyramid, a system of lemon and lavender pastilles anatomizing each rib in the cage, each nib in the pencase, pinnate, for flight, until I am a complete, corrupt authority, embracing my apocrypha and appendices, an encyclical, lie-telling tract. When the novelty of histories is expended, then finally I demonstrate the clean slate, the sponge bath, modesty. I demonstrate a milky or a snowy breast, a white cap with black ribbons like a mourning maid or a morning maid or a young bride surprised by her brother-in-law and made or the watchman or the chaplain. I am cloaked in banality when I succumb and subside.

16. To amuse ourselves, my daughter and I decide to eat only round things, starting with boiled hen's eggs. Roulades and rillettes will be permitted later. Skinned grapes at midday. I remember a bottle of pearl onions, hand-sized and with a waist, and how the onions stared at me, round and dull and not unlike a skinned grape, and not unlike a bad beginning. Now they're in a soldier's hand or gullet, or gazing at nothing in the cupboard of a boarded apartment in a locked-down city. Either way, what a waste!

We concoct a game, sketch a roulette wheel, a target. My daughter holds the paper while standing on a cushion. I toss rolled stockings her way. When I hit any part of the paper, it crackles, then she doubles over, laughing like a queen.

While my daughter is sleeping, I sit at the sill with a worn pack in my hands. Touching me back. We are the same age. I make out his body between two creases in the blackness, two cypresses. What is that third thing that walks between us. His eyes are an empty storeroom, hoarding darkness, as if there could ever be a shortage of that. But his pale, pale face. His pale hands. Are like a signal, agreed upon in advance.

17. I read and reread the movie magazines I brought with me. The poised faces grow more poised, silver eyes more removed as time paces and the pages grow loose.

My lover's reputation has somehow arrived intact with him, though what an artist can mean in such an artless town I can't imagine. He's borrowed the milliner's bicycle and takes little jaunts around the countryside, trading portraits for provisions, whole unsmiling families in their Sunday best beneath a sheaf of wedding silver or a Bible spread to its centerfold. He hems and haws, pretends to take the day, and then finally executes a swift sketch which captures their resemblances and harmonies, the way a genetic melody approaches and departs from itself, a fugue in seven bodies, continuous ink strokes fleeing the sheet. They glimpse briefly at the final product, put it hastily out of sight like the innocently obscene scribblings of a child, then hand over a fatty ham, jar of olives, or sweet ripe cheese. These we eat late at night in small bold bites made complex by the uncertainty of the exchange.

18. One afternoon we are in his studio over the bar-café, rain is falling, and beyond, I am watching a boat rise and fall convulsively on its lead, small as a spitwad dog. The radio confirms that martial law has been declared in the city. Martial law really being a billeting campaign, as the city has been nearly emptied by all but the most patriotic whores who will not desert the capital.

But too late, for the student everyone is looking for, Adeodatus X, has somehow melted away, eroded in the rain which washes all things to the sea. So next the army will be cordoning the sea, that is the seaside, searching internally for the young man, who is said to be of average build, average height, with the same dark hair that is part of God's national design for our brave, buggered *patria*.

19. All the virtual palisades are up, but the virus is mutating, growing gummy claws that can stick to surfaces, working up frog lungs, breaking its own back with snouts and appendages, dividing its eyes, mirroring, overlaying the googlemap with driplines and airstrips with a jellied wildness. No wheel can turn on it; tank treads, stripped from driving a jumble of printer's type, can only offer a spongy porousness to this lump life, pouressness, what could meld there, a tank-tread love motel, a liquid colony, like in the movie where the bunnies dance on water then get down in the decrepit plane, cockpit and bomber-bay full of bunny, bunny mascara and bunny hairspray, bunny thigh and boot, smoke and shield, mutable and decayed, ready to change forms, a green tide, an hide, an ivied ocean which lifts its skirts thigh high. Cry, the lacerate valley, strafe-green with bacterial eyes, how I clawed through to retrieve myself, my palms and arm-bones fronding, my tissue bourgeoning, how I clambered through that change, poke-eyed, stalk brush face, how I met the virus, how I unmathed it under the chops, how I accepted a new life as a hostess, how I changed to live

20. I see my young man all over town like a bright needle surfacing in dull fabric. Sometimes I wonder if I'm dreaming him, pasting him into the scene. Because the crowd folds and parts around him with noone's notice. Noone speaks to him, meets his eye. He does no business. At times he seems produced by the crowd or by the scene, some remainder. Are they avoiding him, in fear of him, ashamed of him? Is he Adeodatus X or a local shepherd, a collaborator or a saboteur, an agent of the army, a nobody, a spy?

I see him one morning before the lavender bushes which hedge a laundry yard. He's eating something hid in his hand, a clammy lavender-green sheen creeping halfway up his cheek. Behind him white sheets snap the wind in surrender or alarm.

21. And the next time in the market, dreamy with heat. He stands in the middle of the scene.

–What's your business here, I ask him.

–What's yours? Buying or selling?

–My price rises with every asking, and high, too high for you.

He raises both hands like a saint. In one, a small notebook wrapped with a leather thong and a silver button. In the other, a tarnished gold watchcase which vibrates on his palm. It pops open to show a little world made cunningly, gears behind a glass plate.

 –Hold it to your ear! he says.

 I do. I feel my teeth and my bones go lacy, little clockwork ants filling my ear canal.

–It's a new kind of metal, very soft. It spreads information.

–Queer sensation.

–Then you're sensitive.

—Impossible, I say, snapping the case shut. You must be thinking of someone else.

—No, it's you I'm thinking of. Why don't we meet at the seaside? Why can't we talk?

Before I can respond my eye catches my daughter at the edge of the market, holding up her skirts. In place of her black boots she is wearing the wooden clogs issued to the urchins of this place. I grab her wrist and begin slapping the back of her neck, meanwhile reaching out to slap the sallow cheeks of the children gathered all around us.

—Where are her shoes? I ask again and again. Where are her shoes? Each face grins at his slap, then flits out of sight. The young man strolls past me, laughing at the wretched little scene.

—*Sabotage.*

22. The seaside graveyard has no kind of lock, not even a gate, but simply a path leading up to where the iron rails parted to admit any comer. My daughter and I find ourselves there one afternoon, each wearing flat straw Sunday hats which seem to support the white fluffy clouds like a tray of buns. I do not take a picture with the ugly Brownie camera my lover is always foisting on us. We climb the sandy trail and look down on the full arm of the bay. The water is an uncertain grey green color, does not look well against the brilliant sky and does not invite reflection. The graveyard is comparatively gay, white and grey stones specked over with a yellow sea moss, the lambs worn to nubs, the angels and obelisks solid but canted to slightly rakish angles by the shifting earth like lanterns for a party. The grass is tough and tall and catches the toe as do the low stones, and the general effect is one of tumbledturveyness despite each headstone's careful accounting of days and months and years. Like water in a sieve, time can't be held in place: it upsets the earth: time all run about and rising.

My daughter examines the front and back of each stone, tracing her fingers through the worn engravings, leaping nimbly among the dead. I sit and drank a bottled lemon, I have to conserve my strength as, like a doctor, I may be called upon to perform at any hour of the night. Studying the little yard, I notice something tucked behind a headstone at the sea edge. A rolled blanket and a small rucksack of boiled wool. I lift the leather thong from its buckle and find a small collection of treasures inside: a hunk of bread, a pocket knife, a folded handdrawn map like a boy would make, and a dirty photo, not as dirty as it might have been, featuring a powdered actress on a photographer's couch. She is past forty, wearing a kind of Cleopatra ensemble: headdress, sandals, snake. I think of keeping it, but tuck it back inside, lest some pimply customer-in-training miss it at his next retreat.

That night in a dream he presses me up against the headstone holding the photo in his hand like a mass card. No teenager but a young man raises his pale face from my shoulder, with its swart singed zero mark, a face made to be lit by moonlight.

The next five o'clock finds me again in the deserted graveyard with only the sea for my companion, dour and whiskery as an old sick aunt. She keeps turning towards and then away from me, too sick to deliver the condemnation on the tip of her lips.

23. Four soldiers arrive in town one Sunday noon when the double doors of the chapel have finally clapped smugly closed. The young soldiers stand somewhat uncertainly on the browned green, their uniforms and skin both varying shades of clam and grime, even their four-wheeled military vehicle looking tinny and anemic. They speak with inland accents and seem unsure of themselves in the presence of so huge and blank a slate as the sea, challenging them to chalk up their lessons before the whole class. Finally, after scanning the sleepy buildings and empty square for some time, they ask in the bar-café for the mayor, who as it happens has repaired here with his wife for a Sunday lunch, wearing his usual brown pin-stripe that hangs all around him like despair. As suits his office, he had been a rotund man—it had been rumored that extra links had been added to the mayoral chain to fit his rounded form—but a dire illness had struck him last year that shrank him down almost to the bone. He has survived like a revenant, though of course he is the self-same man: it's the rest of his flesh gone walking elsewhere. I suppose he will be reunited with it in the next life.

Each Sunday with his still-portly wife he sits down to an outsized meal typical of his former self—fish in cream, meat in gravy, potatoes boiled, baked, fried and gratineed, some limp protesting greenery, cheese and dried fruit and boiled eggs and crackers, a lumpy many-tiered desert, food enough for six hungry travelers. The owner sweats and brings his entire stock of platters to bear on this bounty, and though the wife applies herself like a dignified barnyard creature, the mayor struggles more with every bite, his chin up, his neck distending like a wading bird when swallowing a fish. He gives a greenish look around the cafe at these moments, straining to keep his eyes anywhere but on his plate and the gloomy task of consumption. And when he sees the soldiers he instantly springs up.

The soldiers, mayor, and the owner talk back and forth over the bar. They need rooms in advance of their officer's arrival. It will be no problem; the unrest has hurt tourism, and all the rooms above the bar are empty, save one.

24. Now in my hobble skirt I'm hobbling through heat. It makes a container through which I slot like a thought, too small to disturb. Thick rinds of heat. High-hatted heat. Balloon-blue. Baleen. The smell from the ocean is rank, I begin to go over. My mind swells to touch the pane of the sky and I can see my lover and daughter resting in the shade of a long line of trees, with a basket of apples between them. They could be lovers, but what do lovers mean, but what do lovers let come between them? They could be lovers. I lay that thought away.

The road back to the hotel snakes like the arm of a nerve or a nerve up the arm or a needle in the vein or a microscopic beast which, slipped into the water, makes the water crack and bleed. My room is hot as a grave but I can lock the light away, make a pact with the severe slatted shutters. They stand around smugly in slate grey: *you knew you would need us.* I ignore those stern ladies and strip off my dress, my stockings, my stays, and then I stand at the mirror searching my face for what's written there, my lines.

25. Night falls and my daughter does not return. It does not worry me. She is with my lover, the most inventive and resourceful of men. Their absence sweeps open door after door. Green moonlight fills the room and makes a path from my window down to the stand of pines opposite, slick as a length of film. I pull a green coat over my chartreuse slip, plus stockings and crepe slippers. Then I grab the sill and lower myself down from the window. For no one watching, I cross quickly to the shelter of the pines. The stand is dry and stuffy, like being inside a wooden box of leather gloves, blue, green, black, and brown, but then in a breeze the hands part again and I see the full face of the moon, drunk, distracted, and laughing. Now I'm running like a wraith or bride for the serpentine path that climbs the shallow side of the cliff. The stiff grasses poke and snag at my stockings. My shoes keep sinking into the sand, so I lift them faster. I'm climbing the flat stones that line one side of the walk. They come loose with my weight and I have to keep making little leaps up. When I reach the top, I lose my balance and swing back the way I've come. My two hands hit the dry ground behind me. Light's shining like a dazzling cape laid on the sea. Then one motion grabs the nape of my neck and shines a light into my eyes. I'm blinded, my neck is released and my head hits the sand in a noiseless crash. Bursts on my closed eyes like photographers at a star wedding. I reach out, feel only air, twist around and struggle up to the level. A hand grabs my upper arm and yanks me to my feet. I open my eyes

26. He studies me over a cigarette, leaning against a headstone.

He is a student, and he is the student. Adeodatus. X.

I say you know that soldiers have covered the town.

You know that students have covered the street like a snowfall, each one bleeding from the chest a sweet poppy-colored breath, like life was just a schoolboy phase, now phased out, from breath side to death side like aliens, teen dreams.

You know it's bandtime when it's bedtime, beat the band and beat the sheet, for the last under the duvet is a goose and like a goose stinks and like a goose gets stuck with a dirndl needle up its underside. And like a goose stuffed with the finest sweetmeats. Beats a retreat.

That's the better part of valor. Re-read. Retreat.

He says You know the heart is a piece of valor, a bleeding piece, as the bandolier is an object lesson, and that's why soldiers wear them like vestments, a Greek cross of souls ready to beat a retreat. You know students wear their souls in those black bags, straps that cut their chests. You know a student pedaled up to a group of soldiers on his rusting bike and blew the pack of them up. You know the little settlement of students was razed and dozed into the sea. You know the tangle of student's bones forms the skeleton of a huge whale, a hungry whale that nonetheless choked on the bone in his own throat.

I take out a cigarette, and as he leans forward to light it our reciprocal wrists lock in a moment of twinship, symmetry. Comrade, I say, wrinkling my nose at the homely word. As I smoke I think about damage and lucidity. I gaze upwards at the absentminded night, puttering around its chamber in its loose dark robe, hardly noticing the colony of rodents scrabbling here below.

27. The mayor gathers us on the green with three of the soldiers—the fourth not present, which causes a thin needle of apprehension to work the brows of those gathered. I try to remember what he looked like, but can only bring to mind those standing before us in canvas jackets, berets, and Jeep-grey trousers tucked in to sagging boots: one looks like another.

The mayor stands before us in an even more abject state than usual, his arms flapping in his huge sleeves.

—Dear citizens, do you need me to tell you what you already *know*? Have you been attending to the fate of our dear nation as is the patriotic duty of your *soul*? Are you aware that she is imperiled and has been so savaged by recent events that she is racked to her daybed and can not get *up*? So that we all must stand up for *her*? That this student, I cannot bring myself to say his name, it is such a puny name, the name of a flea or tick which I look forward to personally pinching and burning to nothingness, yes, I will wield the civic tweezer and the civic match, could be in our very *midst*? That these soldiers have formed a kind of sack around the countryside with its open mouth protruding towards this very town, this very *promontory*? That they are about to set their very boots onto this sack, as on a goose's bladder, and force the scoundrel out of hiding and into our waiting *arms*? That of all towns in the patria it has fallen to *us* to play this vital role, due to the extreme bareness, or shall we say the frankness, of our *coastline?* That the break could come at any *time?* And surely it is transparently the case that any strangers in our midst are to be referred to the town hall, which will now be open day and night and manned by myself, my spouse and these fine young boys, whose apparent strength reflects the nourishing vitality of our country's very bosom, in aid of which it is our great honor to serve as flexible extremities who are perfectly willing to expend ourselves in our efforts to restore and *defend?*

Under this torrent of interrogatives, some villagers clap vigorously, others uncertainly, others weep or raise inflamed fists. The sun burns through the pale morning mask of clouds. The green stalks stand up expectantly and are mashed down by the hooves of the departing crowd. As the green clears, I catch sight of my daughter and my lover on the edge of the square, she in a man's overcoat, fawn-colored, which folds all about her with improbable lightness, he in the peasant's garb he has lately, irritatingly, taken up. They look so small from here. It is as if a series of ballet sets had been pulled into the wings to reveal, at the very back of the stage, and at the edge of vision, the two lovers posed for a *pas de deux*, poised on the edge of some metamorphosis or catastrophe, on the shoreline of chemical lake, its surface just stirred by the first syllables of a killing gas, a motile evisceration.

28. I fall asleep to the radio and my dreams are cured in music and advertisements and serials and sermons and news. Let's gather round our fosses all the shades that mother nylon has to bless: nude, peach, sunset, nude beach sunset, ebony, mahogany, ma vie in blanc, ma vie en brink, in the drink, Marianne, your tit droite's showing, and a good part of your gauche. Here on the rooftop we have Euro-style toplessness, and for symmetry a second moon, here in L'Auberge Automaton, which is a dead hotel, modeled on the chambers of the nightingale's heart, the ballroom its eyemarl, the float pool its flight bones, and the flightless wings its wings. Let's all gather at the todespiano for a spiel a carol a canon a spell

Nikolai Nightingale, you're such a drag drag drag
O Nikki Nightingale you're such a drag drag drag
You're the angel of the trenches but you're really such a hag

Nikolai Nightingale you're such a sham sham sham
Nikolai Nightingale you're such a sham sham sham
You clutch your sacred heart like it's a stolen ham

Crack a knucklebone you'll find a gem gem gem
Crack a knucklebone you'll find a gem gem gem
On a corpse or on a copse its all the same same same

I fell asleep in Kansas and awoke in Kansas, France. The city had shifted around me. I had been a high school student and was now a student of design. *A tout a l'heure*, I had designs. I harbored them, fondled every ship, its wallet bulge, its prow. Had a good lead on diesel till the price went flop. When the prince went down, I tipped my hat, farewell to princelings, and goodbye tuteleur, I took my lit-rit-cher for a ride, the pages mouldering, I bore them like a termite bore the cross, they say the bugs that bored the true cross shat gems, that made for ruby diadems, that kissed the brows of Russian princesses that dropped down flat to find them in the snow, oh, from their bosoms tipped the o(r)dor of the rose, the ordure of the glen, and their bare bosoms bore the secret any citizen should know, the larval truth, tubercular truffles, a knit truce between myself and my self-same scar, a tissue, a lady's rag tucked in the cuff, expiring at the scene, sacerdotal, I lift this burnt offering which makes a smoke ring, laminate, a killing scent, an unequal march, a waltz with a drop step, a drop stitch, a chainlink a fit in the square a fist in the lip a list a tryst a Liszt a triste Nikolai Nightingale you're such a drag drag drag You sulk like you're a woman but you're really just a Nikolai Nightingale I knew you well well well you played the maid of heaven but you made the beds in

29. We go on living in the small town at the mouth of the trap, waiting for the boot to come down and drive the air out and into our grasping hands. Every townsperson is mobilized to perform the search, performances on the town green that repeat again and again, everyone getting a turn at the starring role. The mayor ties a hammock of hay around his belly, his wife brings down a set of folded-away shirts to button over his restored girth, and sets the papier mache head on his shoulders that my lover has mocked up with the features of Adeodatus X. A long snaky line disgorges itself onto the green: the milliner, the milliner's son, the baker, the milking girls—and the townspeople stepped onto the stage in fiver-person cadres, representing Suspicion, Detection, Pursuit, Resolve and Action, this latter person usually the weakest and smallest of the group, driving the bayonet into the mayor's padded gut to comic effect.

As a constant, I play the part of the nurse, done up in an apron and a kind of veil. Each actor brings the real symbols of their professions with them—wheat sheaves, churns, measuring tape and pins, the wetnurse her bare breast and nappy. The idea is to demonstrate the commitment of every hand in the village to the vigilance. As they climb onto the rostrum, I hand out the necessary props: a bible for the maiden to grasp, a skirt for Adeodatus to violate, a wooden gun with the real bayonet to be wielded by the frailest hands. And so the pageant adapts itself again and again, the script the same but the figures growing fat and bent and scrawled and sturdy, the same word drawn by hand after hand after hand.

30. It appears our efforts at reinvention and readiness recapitulate in miniature the revolutions going on in other sectors of the country. After our hard labors all the dusty day, we gather in the bar cafe, the mayor with the hay still matted by sweat to the small of his back, his fat wife quite exhausted, I in my apron and veil, my head marked with a cross. We hand around icy glasses and in silence we watch a livid footage cycle on the screen, Adedodatus X landing at an airstrip, climbing a rostrum, greeting children through a window, silhouetted against a sky gangrenous with plane tracks. We can't know from what angular and well-lit universe these images are cast, nor its distance in time and space from the end to all such images, the demise we have so thoroughly rehearsed. We look around for the soldiers for information and advice but they have slipped out from among us. Then the crowd started splits off too, the women and small children, the unmarried girls, until it's just me and the barmaid and the cluster of men slumped in their ill-fitting getups like a single shucked glove, a half-gesture, the fingers of an uncommitted hand.

31. I love a little dog in this town. Its face is white, its coat is a rusty caramel, it appears to be wearing little trousers as it waddles antically around the benches outside the bar cafe. For a crust it goes up on its hindlegs and for a beer it turns. Apparently going up on its hindlegs is not an unknown pastime for this creature because around the town and even out on some of the farms one can see the results of its amorous adventures, little rust colored sprigs of hair and squat haunches marking the whelps of boxer and German shepherd and Doberman and even poodle bitches. I like having this little fellow nearby, and everyone reports his activities to me, calling him 'your dog'. I tie my ribbon in its matted neck.

This town has made me sentimental as a milkmaid, or a mayor's wife.

But perhaps such fancies are the product of an otherwise sharpened mind. For myself, my lover, and even my daughter have been changed by contact with this occupation, like touching one's hand to a hot wire. My lover is employed making images of the fugitive, on paper and parchments, sheets hung from lines, wire sculptures that can be fitted with a bulb and hung up like lanterns, papier mache kiosks pulled by bicycle, masks and props for the drills, little badges to be worn by boys, he's even partnered with local artisans in a ceramic enterprise, studying the local clay, forms, paint, and kilns. And so the student's face multiplies till it is everywhere, pale cheek, black mark, black eyes, black curl.

32. My daughter has exerted herself in no other way but to grow, and so she too is serving the occupation like all the other young girls in the town, by hovering on the edge of her womanhood and sharpening the imaginative faculties of the young soldiers. Her affection for the wooden clogs and white chemises of the local waifs has disappeared, and now she acquits herself with dresses from my own wardrobe, close cut and becoming, and the little angled hats around which I set her hair in curls. I have seen the raised eyebrows this draws from the local matrons as she tacks behind me like a little ship, my Niña, and it's said I have corrupted her which is neither true nor fair. Life corrupted her like a poisoned lake, life like a poison gas. While other moths dress their daughters in the palest shades of funeral flesh I dress mine in chemical colors that soldiers understand.

This is how the occupation has sharpened both myself and my daughter. Sharpened our little claws.

33. The singlemindedness of summer has turned the village fixed and stiff, like a mask that sits on a table. It does not animate the table. A strained uneventfulness adheres to the contours of the town like another condition of summer. We cling to the seaside again. The water that collects in little pools is so mild, unbearably mild, that one begins to question where one's flesh ends and the world's begins. Seaweeds are cooked in this mess, and little fish flit knowingly. Local urchins are out here digging for mussels in the muck. They tuck huge slimy hanks of seaweed into the brims of their hats like monstrous braids or fling it at each other with a shower of scum. An ambient electric greenness frays from these adornments and wraps itself around a wrist or an ankle. The children fight, sharpen sticks and poke each other, develop and abandon affections as casually as turning cards back into the mill of the deck. Meanwhile the fish in the tidepool chase their own shadows like an antic clock and the solid, unadvancing heat makes the afternoon stutter.

Between us my daughter and I share a plate of peaches which we eat down to the pit, revealing an inky profile, chin, nose, birthmark, cap. This man. As if the whole shallow dish of the world were made for him.

34. After months of desertion, the capital is suddenly boiling over with people. The center of that town erupts with fists like a bulb forced open by the maggots inside. A man stands up on the roof of a car and addresses the crowd. The camera draws in close—this is no student. His grey hair brushes back from his face, he wears black glasses and an open-collared striped blue shirt. He could be a laureate for literature or the owner of a chain of car washes, but he clambers onto the roof of the car with a bullhorn in his hand for amplification that can't radiate more than a few feet. The chanting crowd waves green placards stenciled with this man's face in white paint.

In the bar cafe, the soldiers have been eating sandwiches and studying the screen. Static erupts from upstairs as the soldiers' radio suddenly comes alive. One jumps up to receive the transmission and the others go outside to have a smoke and continue tinkering with their vehicle. With the soldiers gone, the place feels looser and the various posters and flyers, handbills and carvings of Adeodatus X all have sightlines on one another, black eye to black eye. I open a paper fan featuring his visage and flutter it once. Then we all sit frozen, watching the demonstration, where another face multiflorates in the upraised, multiplying hands.

35. Composition or charisma? With the works of this hand-carved clock now frozen in shock, the cuckoo's beak pried permanently open to reveal neither worm nor jewel, we step outside the operation of the plot for a technical discussion. My lover leans against the stone wall for a short cigarette, his cupped hand shading it from the ether. His fingers are stained black, he wears thick boots like a working man, and he is now, at last, a working man, producing images of Adeodatus by the gross, pound, bushel and bale. A light mist is falling; I feel my lashes matte prettily, my brown hair curl, my blue-grey cycling costume begin to cling. Composition or charisma? Which one makes for the truer art? It is not so simple as to search out synonyms—technique or inspiration, say, or craft or vision. These are lesser dichotomies, fit for the accountant's books. Whereas composition and charisma exist in the world like Hindoo deities, they are non-comparable, though for our purposes we will attempt to compare. Composition may be taught, while charisma cannot be acquired; but charisma may be useless, despite its many lovely palms, each representing an attribute, the precise disposition of its waist, neck, or fingers, the tongues of fire that leap from its maiden skull. My lover will not stand for useless art (though he has always supported my uselessness). His art responds (and he has always relied on my responsiveness). Art must be in and of the world. But it is this responsiveness that is,

perhaps, charisma, a liqui-solvent materium that melts to many atavistic forms. Political yet set on the ideal, forgiving yet zealous, its mutability is a kind of absolutism, its capaciousness a grating permanence. This I do not say, as I watch the beads of rain collect in the metal grid of my bicycle basket, glut the spokes. As I watch the chain count its teeth, turned out of its mouth as if by fate's celestial truncheon, now strung up as an adornment. The rain arrives through the luciferous ether, along with the light. It blurs as it clarifies, it concentrates as it disperses. It carries a valise of little value, though folded inside are metals and toxins divers as a magpie's hoarde, which pierce the pores and lie down in the chromosome, to pout and fume, rout and get fat.

36. Later, dozing in my lover's sheets, which are filthy with charcoal, paint, graphite, wax and wine, I dream into a dark blue vault, in which I spot the wooden bird flying fitfully, knocking about in the eaves for an exit, its eyes painted wide and unable to close. It sees me and turns to me its pried open beak. And I too float or fly forward to peer inside that tiny hinged orifice, and then I am inside, where all is black and gelatinous, and I like an avatar glide on, with one fist forward, the fist locked behind me at the small of my back, signifying resolve. The body of this bird is more capacious than it had ever looked, and lightless, and my eyes are completely blinded as I punch forward with my lifted fist. Matter cakes and flows from my eyes, face and mouth. I'm choking. I open and close my fist experimentally, to see if I can breathe through it. My lungs fill. My arm is now my throat. If I can keep moving forward, I'll close my hand around the jewel in this bird's gullet. My wrist will swallow it. Then I'll be the bird. I'll turn myself inside out and make a pendant of this bit of bile, my heart.

37. On the second day of demonstrations supporters un-
furl a huge stitched banner from one side of Rectitude
Square to the other. In an endless red field, two hares
locked in a mirrored wardrobe. Legend: to cure their
harebrainedness and restore their memories. Shards of
mirrors, blood, scrabbling claws, tufts of hair are ren-
dered in wax relief on the red red cloth. Hares, don't you
know they love to multiply, or be cut up like poets so
that their influence spreads (disjecta membra) or like
mercury spores scattered through the home, decorate the
brain, a cure for evil thoughts. Nuns and grandmothers
take to the brutalist offices of the government, using their
fingers, skilled at sifting beans and beads, and their sharp
eyes, skilled at ferreting out guilty thoughts, to piece back
together the ripped and shredded documents that lazy
clerks left in the bins. So far their efforts have only reaped
flawed budget reports, but these they hoist like bloody
shirts. Normal life has scarcely resumed in the rest of
the city, which is about a quarter filled with people pry-
ing sepulchres of dust and filth from their apartments.
Some homes were used for billeting, with soldiers turning whole rooms into latrines, though others were apparently occupied by oddly fastidious types, and housewives
move through these scrubbed and brightened halls with
both gratitude and unease, for the presence of such an
coruscating hand lingers, it lingers. Brigades clean out
the shrines, farmers trepidaciously enter squares with

vegetables wilted less from the heat than from uncertainty. The city continues to fill. The Holiday Inn blunts its bright wishes into the sky, evening shots occasionally pitching yellow, red, or green in its orisons.

One can assume the Holiday Inn never abandoned its convictions as, unlike the stunted university hospital, it has its own generator, which is the same as faith.

38. My lover is certain the soldiers will leave. Like all of us, they are drawn like needles towards the capital, the heart of the country, but they have the freedom of their uniforms and can travel the arteries and lodge in that heart. They are restless; he has heard them moving about the inn all night, and he himself has also been busy dragging canvases, fliers, posters of Adeodatus X down to the cellar, stacking and tying them neatly by materials and date of execution. My lover is a man who believes in legacy, who foresees a future that mirrors this one like a more beautiful twin, a future whose arrival one must ready for with discipline, grooming, order, and commitment. Like a man clearing a plot of land, this gives him a method with which to subdue the present, which for the rest of us is just now clotted and hovering like an augur spilling its gore and guts from a slit belly into our brows and cheeks and hair. It weighs our eyes nearly shut, which draws the world in sharply, as if we were peering at the day through a jewel, or through the tracks of an image cut on the face of a jewel, a combat diamond.

39. Girls who fancy themselves the sweethearts of these soldiers gather at the mouth of the inn, homely white lace kerchiefs tied up in their hair, half imagining that the soldiers will sweep them up into the departing Jeeps. There are a few more of them than the soldiers—who knows which of them has cherished a passing glance, a morning greeting, a touch of hands over a full or empty bucket of milk, and which of them has performed a demonstration of true country pleasures in barn or field or in the blank of some stream.

My daughter, who has been if not the sweetheart then the *nonparielle* of each of these boys in turn, is nowhere to be seen. I believe she is back at our guest house, sleeping in. She is cultivating a disciplined lassitude these days which is practical in our profession and also quite becoming. For sleep is the inverse of money; like air and water, they can't exist in the same place. This is why whores are always awake at night, ever vigilant, even more so than the soldiers, policemen, and prison guards who love us and whose pockets we rob. And yet I can sleep at any hour— just as I can also make money. I snatch each when I can.

Sometimes I think I am as rulebound as a nun; indeed, they transferred their discipline to me through a steady tattoo on the backs of my thighs when I was a girl in their care. And, indeed, it is in this exact bit of flesh where my lover likes to tie thick ribbons, apply the weight of his hand.

The seat of knowledge.

40. Anyone listening hears the departure, just at dawn. An engine catches, flimsy doors slam shut, boots stamp, gears shift, a toy-sized motor glides like a fly for the carcass of the capital, suddenly revived. That corpse sits up, with marl-white eyes and drowned black locks. Her limbs and arteries jerk with the unexpected animation of a thousand flies, her face cakes in dismay. Meanwhile, in the countryside, day fastens her blue girdle over the whole affair and turns to us a bland impassive face. Day within day. The soldiers have left their maps and other relics of the manhunt in their rooms. Stamps of his face dot the countryside and coastline, here circled in orange wax crayon, here crossed out, here ringing a fat promontory like a gartered thigh. I have seen these maps before, nearly transparent, pinned up at town meetings where we were divided into details for supply and search or reported our nil findings. Whereas on those occasions they represented a plan advancing, a plot climbing for its peak, now they amount to a littering of markings without priority, a record of fruitless tasks.

By midday my daughter joins me in a travelling suit whose color might best be described as citrine or 'Disdain'. For this girl carries a bitter tang, a lime rind preserve. I am dressed in a costume whose evident components suggest the animals it derives from: whalebone, ostrich, hare. The day is perverse, having sunk from a bland summer blowsiness to a white funk blown in off the sea, colorless and offputting as the eye of a crone. The fog submerges exteriors and permeates interiors; the inn is slick and thin as the chambers of a frog's heart. The mayor and his wife have arrived and are greeting concerned and addled citizens here. The mayor eats nothing for his lunch, but the wife seeks to counter the clamminess of the day by ordering every possible gelee the inn can muster—shellfish terrine, foie gras entier en gelee, rabbit gelee and balottine, chicken liver mousse with grape gelee. We're fascinated with this meal which sweats and wobbles on the table; many of these dishes are moulded to the form the unfortunate animals took in life, and equally unctuous is the pleasure with which the mayor's wife splits and hashes these pretty forms with her tiny fork. She barely acknowledges the constituents who come to discuss the departure of the army and the uncertainty of the day. 'Anyway you have to eat' more than one comments solicitously, and she cuts her eyes at them like the flat of a knife, its business-end pointed elsewhere.

41. I am beginning to like the mayor's wife, who exists, after all, in a world of her choice, lace beribboned avenues of the choicest fat. My daughter and I order strawberries and sour cream and toast her (without her knowledge) as we down the slick and sour contents. It's like eating something already half digested by a beast of the field. We chortle as it nearly gags us.

This bad day sticks in the throat and will not pass.

Meanwhile, on the screen, tear gas, fires, a scrim of blood that lowers over a young woman's forehead like a special effect. The two symbols of this movement—the grey-beard's stenciled face and the pulled apart hares, are hung from balconies, tied to faces, slung over garments, or burned in the hands of livid reactionary gangs. Although we search every news cycle for the face we have trained ourselves to see in any crowd, setting, context, against light or dark curtain or oceanic backdrop, we never see the student. We never see him. It would seem our village villain has become completely obsolete.

With the soldiers gone, the town cannot return to its former orientation; it twists like a wilting balloon. On the second day, this listlessness is assuaged by ripping up banners, crashing ceramic mugs and platters, burning up piles of effigies that otherwise would have sustained one night's bonfire. The scene briefly reprises those in the capital—a cloud of vicious fume, a mocked up massacre—and like a funerary rite, all actions bend toward waste and expenditure. But what death are we mourning?

I must admit I am feeling fine amid the tumult. The crashing and ripping, the fumes and smoke, the capricious violence nicely fills the little bowl of the day like a raucous ballroom on the Apocalypse. All the demons want to play. I feel so light amid this chaos, like it could lift me straight to heaven on its upraised hands or a cunning trapeze, fixed to the celestial vaults, yea, and I a burlesque Joan of Arc, my costume conveying ultra nakedness with its sequined bodice like a sprinkle of champagne-colored stars, a skirt split at the knee and trailing, nylon starlight as the trapeze rises like a sigh.

Then even the violence breaks like a toy (and indeed it has no more significance). Everything that may be broken or burned has been broken and burned. It is late afternoon, and the flushed and tired faces find their succour not only at the inn, but in the drawing rooms that line the square. Night refuses to fall, and the anticness becomes more forced. An edge of violence returns to the proceedings. My daughter and I retreat to the studio to watch this welcome transformation through the wide window. My daughter wears a clever sized-down top hat, striped in circus colors and black velvet. It perches high and rakishly in her teased high hair as if thrown back by shock, though what could shock us? As if thrown back in pleasure. My daughter, it is clear, has been pursuing her friendship with the young son of the milliner. Evidently, he is possessed of quite nimble fingers.

My Rat

1. My daughter has been sleeping in my office, 24/7, 2, 3, 4 nights in a row. It's too dangerous for her to wake up and go home. I want to bundle her into a taxi in a bedsheet and whisk her off to the greenzone. But there's no home or zone so here she sleeps with the candi-colored videofeed flitting over her forehead, over her fleecy sleeper-shoulder, above where the honey bear is stitched, on the wall above her crib which is a cubicle, an office-style bunker, swaddled with post-it notes.

Above the weatherfeed, the Great Bear rolls over, which gave its name to the Arctic, also the Antiarctic, and also the Little Bear, first H- dropped on Nagasaki, H'Nagasaki, honey bomb of sleep, unitybomber, cancer comb that sinks its teeth into the bone

bred there and bored there
combing her aubrun hair there
in the cancerscape, in the traumazone
I've never been to hiroshima

never again never stopped happening
my daughter's voice is a rattle
a vespa called marinetti unzippers Rio
the coffeenut zips a comb between its teeth
the brazil nut sinks like a wooden boat falling apart mid-
flight from the Nazis
with all hands on
with no eyes screwed up rotting and crying
the searchbeam of history dripping by
I heard a fly when I
unzipped the image from the drive
Iago imago sunk a dagger in my eye the toothed pixel cut
the zippy comb
sang as it sank rainbow rainbow rainbow
the killed medieval baby
through its cut throat
laughed and danced on the sky
and S.O.S.'d
and radio'd
and then I let the fish go
and then I heard the fly die

Grazie, graziela, gradisca, lagniappe, four-eyes, you were
my something-for-nothing, lets go to the videofeed, to
the fanzone, to the cyclotron of water lilies, waterhoses,
-spouts and –boards and -jets, the twisted t-shirt which
hoards the drip, let's feel our genetrip rip apart and get
suspended in gravid jelly, jellied gravity, let's take a cat-
nap in the hairtrap, let's hear it for survival, daisycutter,
fogcutter, esophageal trip, rip, unzipped inlet repositories,
deposits gnawing and kneading a gallstone lustrous with
pearly liqueur, that'll have to come up, that'll have to come
out, that'll be a lifeline for steering by how it catches the
water so queerly as it rolls on the moonlit deck

time to flip the trip
time to turn the page
read-a-long was our antique flag
pre-deathphage-sur-la-plage   turn
and now my daughter sleeps on the information deck
she sleeps on soft knowledge on the hard hard drives

2. At about 1 AM our Interlocutor shows up. I move my
daughter to a blanket-lined laundry basket in the hallway, seat our Interlocutor at my desk. I steady the lights,
trigger the camera, settle a headset on our Interlocutor's
head. I settle his head to the rest. I begin the feed. Our
Interlocutor begins moving his mouth along to the words
that flit by on the screen. I tap him twice on his arm and

he raises a finger. Then I gently close the door behind me and sit with my daughter in the hall.

After an hour he leaves, and I move my daughter inside again. She's warm in the heat from the instruments, and the glow. The dials and indicators leap and flip like candlelight where she's curled up.

Just before dawn she wakes up. I gather her into my arms and we sit down together in our Interlocutor's seat. It feels just vacated as if by a cat. I feel his body around me as I hold my daughter. Her eyes are open, she is poking a tiny finger at the vented back of the chair, dragging her nail through its stipple. Scratch, scratch, scratch, this is how the organism enters into the bloodstream, how my daughter enters into knowledge.

3. We go out onto the roof to breathe in the shade of our laundry. The sky's uncertain, waiting in a line of skies, holds a claimcheck with an inscrutable sign. Holds it without looking, at its side. Drifts it down below the line. It occurs to me to be more didactic with my daughter, I say, "These are your ears. These are your ankles," and her eyes fill with that amusement which is a form of resistance. I scoop her up in her basket and take her inside to a custodian's closet with a deep square sink for washing off mops and filling buckets. The closet is remote enough

that noone has found it and converted it to a pissoir or worse; I sit my daughter in the trough and let a trickle of water weave around her shoulders. I start again: "These are your toes, and these are your ankles." She waves a straight-armed palm at me without looking up; she is listening to the water groan in the tap.

4. That night she is asleep and aflame when our Interlocutor arrives again. He's early; it's just before midnight. The dials and the arrows dip and dip again like a waitress taking a weight onto her shoulder, then straighten up. I put my daughter in her basket and place it at my feet, roll back our Interlocutor's chair but this time rather than sit down he closes two fingers on my shoulder; they reticulate like two hooks. They never leave my back as a I crouch down for my daughter, stand up and am steered into the hall. Here a thin hot tube of light slithers over the doorway, casting almost no light beyond itself. Our Interlocutor guides me down the hall to the door that opens up onto a sheer banked wall of night. Air licks in at us as I push my foot out onto the small rectangular grate. I know this escape well from climbing up to the roof each morning. Now I am climbing down, gripping the metal where it has melted and refused like a scoliotic spine. I loosen my grip to slip over the thinnest strips and gratefully clutch the thicknesses. My Interlocutor descends above me, his greater weight causing the helical structure to half-twist from side to side. The counterweight of my

daughter speeds my own turning, and the three of us make an astronomical cycle plummeting to earth. The sky sickens, goes pea green, settles to black again.

On the jagged cement our Interlocutor guides me by his grip; it is absolutely lightless, but I am turned to the right, to the left, moved down a step. What guides him. There is a noise of steel-headed locks flying upwards (sleepers, awake!) and a lacquered door swings outward, just catching the rubber edge of the basket. I try to tighten my hold. In the light from the interior I see that my daughter is awake and watchful. I put the basket on the seat and keep one hand on it as I climb in, nudging it over with my weight. Our Interlocutor climbs in next, clunks a night-vision-enabled mask at his feet. I can't see a driver. The engine follows the instruments on a dashboard, we are a compact drone moving over the streets which by day look deserted, by night form a roiling invisible market of masked and goggled Interlocutors, targets and hunters, a tide of rival signs.

5. We are moving but what do we move through? Thicket of time, a thickness of present-tenseness which sieves me and renders me reactive matter. I am ready to seize my daughter and crush her to me, hope that when death seizes us he will seize us together and directly into his lightless interior and spare us the threshold of human hands.

In my right periphery is the profile of our Interlocutor, and beyond him like a fleck in the film is a hop of light, a little sugary rim that calcifies and deposits and grows harder and larger until I realize it is a vernally lit pavilion at which we anchor. With almost no experience of a threshold the three of us are inside a red reception hall gushing and throbbing with steamy heat and round globes of incandescent light which light the shabby velvets and worn mirrors with relentless cheerfulness. Behind a walnut counter a single uniformed man is attending, theatrically, to some matter below our line of sight. As we approach, he makes a show of noticing us, tilting his head back to reveal huge false upper teeth which he raises like a hatbrim to greet us.

What a person will buy in the black market. What withstands when 90 percent of the population cannot:

vanity.

6. The man behind the desk swats a button like a fly and an elevator begins to labor from below and push into sight behind a brass grate. This hotel, snoozing like an antigen in the city's adipose, has somehow survived the leveling intact, to bloom in the distaster-drome, and so we are shuttled through an exhumed ritual of movement utterly foreign to our usual days of scurrying over, around, and

under our building. We ride up a few floors, one thick dial turning effortfully over over our heads like s story about the sun. We exit the elevator into a hallway with a carpet so thick it swallows our motion. Moving down the length of this overlit hall takes the remainder of the night. A bolt turns over and our Interlocutor plunges into the dark room and rakes back a drapery to reveal an intact plate of glass, and behind it the day wincing as it wakens, a bruise-colored morning. Somewhere during the journey to this point in time my daughter has fallen asleep. I set her basket down between the bed and the interior wall, then sit down on the bed. Our Interlocutor sits down next to me. He pushes my coat aside and we have sex once with our clothes on, and then he wants me to take off my clothes and we have sex again. I am completely naked for the first time in a very, very long time and the heat in the room embraces me. On top I notice for the first time the mirrors hung above the headboard and over the desk opposite, mirrors that propose an infinity of me and then one evacuated of me in the next instant.

When he gets up and leaves the room I take my daughter into the bed and we stretch out under the blankets, but she cries until I put her back in her basket. I sleep for awhile with one hand dangling over the edge and resting on the rubber. He returns (someone returns?) and we have sex again and he leaves. Then I get out of bed. It's afternoon. I pull chains, flip switches, and reach under shades and up spines to find the knobs and twist. I'm able to turn on five separate lights. I open three sliding doors and find two closets and a little bathroom. One of the closets is packed floor to ceiling with clothing—folded, stacked tight, thicknesses of shirts, pants, parkas. The other closet is about shin-high in shoes, all jumbled together, mens and womens. I think about selecting a pair, then leave it. The bathroom is dry and cold and no water runs from the faucets, but there are three sealed liters of water propped against the mirror. I wake up my daughter and feed her a drink, splash a little in her face for a treat. She looks at herself in the mirror.

7. I consider leaving the hotel.

8. I pull on my clothes and coat and sit down to wait the edge of the bed. My daughter crawls in circles on the bed, lies flat and touches her cheek to a pillow, then leaps back to her knees a breath later. She makes an antic clock.

9. Our Interlocutor returns. He's brought with him a few cans of food, the same stuff he leaves in my office, no wrappers, stamped with a serial number on the top. "Do you want to go back to the building or stay here?"

"You stay here?" My own voice sounds bent through a crooked flue. I only use it to speak to my daughter, and then I don't always speak out loud.

"In different rooms."

"Is it safe?" I look at all the lights burning in the room, look right into the bulbs then watch the white walls ulcerate.

"Safer. So far noone comes out this far, not in big enough numbers."

"What about the videofeed?"

"I can do it myself. I'll bring you back there if you want."

"You can do it yourself?"

"Sure."

"Just tonight."

"Sure. But I won't be around." When he gets up and leaves, I work a can open and sniff at the contents. Salty, slippery greens. I open another: orange slices brined in something so sharp and sweet I think it might not be quite right anymore. I spoon up some of the greens on my fingers and feed them to my daughter. She chokes a bit; I consider chewing them for her in my own mouth but then she gets them down. I turn off all the lights and settle in the bed and feel the heat close over us. The sun slinks down and its briny orange smell reaches its fingers over from the other side of the hotel and night fills up the room with the sound of gas moving through the walls. It's like being tucked up in a bomb. We might blow apart in our sleep. Anything touches us, we might blow apart.

10. Somehow we sleep through to morning, both of us, and our Interlocutor does not return. The heat has turned and the room is rank. I pick my daughter up out of her basket, strip her, pour water over her in the sink. It's a sin, potable water to wash an infant's ass. I open the second bottle and drink right from the tip polluting the whole thing. I might be drunk this morning, maybe. I pull a couple shirts out of a closet, wipe my baby dry with one, knot the other around her. I leave her dirty things like peels on the bathroom floor. I'll wash them later, if I can find some more water. Nothing can be wasted. Not even my life, now that I have her.

It's night before our Interlocutor appears in the room. Sitting on the bed, he looks older than when I last saw him. My daughter is pulling herself up by the drawer-pulls in the desk; she falls and bangs her temple on an open drawer, then her head on the leg of the bed. Our Interlocutor wears his hair in an outgrown military cut, he wears an overcoat like undergrowth, he turns his head like the faces of a coin: heads, heads. I tell him I want to go back to my office, and there's a knock at the door. It's a younger man in a leather blazer, black turtleneck, black watchcap, and his job is to take my daughter and me back. The stubble on his face is like flies on milk. I leave the hot room in one motion and hope that our Interlocutor's rank will somehow transfer to me and my daughter, vouchsafe us a smooth transfer. The vehicle churns like a ruminant's gut and the young man watches us climb the escape, as far as halfway.

We sleep the rest of the night through in my office. But I'm worried, now that two men know we're here.

11. The next morning I watch a clutch of gulls knot and pull loose over the east precincts of the city. I peer into squared off ash in every direction and wonder where I was last night, where I could sift to find the crown, that golden tooth. The next morning white missiles fall to the west like paper airplanes, spilled pills, mail or cigarettes dumped out on a bed. Nothing knocks me down, but I sit down hard. I don't know what part of my body is taking the blows.

12. Our Interlocutor does not come back.

13. Reckon our resources: daily trickle of water (from what reservoir?), occasional rain thick with particulate, extra t-shirts, extra shoes I snatched from the hotel, which fit neither of us, a case of mismatched cans (thank god) we open at the rate of one per day that makes for about 23 days left if I don't eat.

23 days. After which something else will come along.

14. But I figure wrong. It's only a handful of days before we're out on the roof and something flies by us. A bird, a bullet, an ash-gorged insect flying hot on the wing.

Back down to my office where the formerly companionable squeaking of the rats in the walls is now shrill and inscrutable.

I'm convinced they know. I'm convinced they know. What's coming next. How we've been haughty, how pride goeth before it goes.

Pride goeth daydreaming in its spit-shone vehicles, a double-motorcade progressing forward and backwards, pulling thin at the middle, lacquered black, viscous and then nothing.

Put on new shoes to greet him, that's a proverb, blind
him briefly with your spit-shone reflectors, take your
switchblade, polished coins, take your pocket protector.

15. Up on the roof again. My daughter drags four fingers
through a puddle but keeps her thumb tucked up. Her
clothes barely fit her. Somehow her bones are growing.
Soon she'll be too heavy to lift up and down the escape.

We're going to have to come down off the roof, soon.
We're going to have to come down off the roof, soon
Out of the building and into the street.
Or what will we eat, what will we eat.
And when we do we'll be seen.
And when we do we'll be a scene.
And when we do we'll have to be dressed as the scene or
the street
Or else we'll be seen
Or else we'll be seen
Taken into the market of death clothes and meat

Or what will we eat. What will we eat.
Rat served with cat. Cat served with rat.
Infants curled up in the cold tureen

Cream separate, the soup growing skin.

And the second skin is the darkness
And the second scene is the building
And the second scene takes place in the tureen
Inside the baby inside the tureen

What do the rats in this building eat.

The opera house, the avenue, the elephants at the zoo,
came swanning up to their deaths, met death at the tip of a
rat's nose, the paintings in the Louvre, all those mountains
and apples and bosoms, the river like a necklace of fat, the
blousy *bois* like the upturned skirts of girls, the loaves and
the *livres*, the cobbles and the cannon, the fodder and the
cannonfodder, the peaked caps and the flat caps and the
brimless caps and the Phrygian caps and the mob caps
and the crowns and the cradle caps, the wimple and the
headwrap, the paper fastfood cap and the hairnet and
the sailor's tam-o-shanter, and the sailor's cut-the-wind,
and the sailor's soupbowl, and the soup tureen, and the
i.v. stand, and the plant stand, and the ivy, the wrought
iron and the pasteboard and the baseboards and the
wainscoting and the drainpipes and the hip roof and
the balustrade and the finials and the gargoyles and the
shingles and the widow's walk and the golden rooster who
sits on top who can only crow as the crow flies as the wind
is blowing and you don't need a weathercock to know
which way to know which way I've got the videofeed but

it's foreign currency it's nothing local I can't look at me the old corporate spy satellites that could tell you five hamburgers within easy walking are dismantled now and rolled over to the other side of the sky at night our city looks like a night sky over a city that is without any stars and in this galactic blackness this lactic elasticity we roll some mammal's complicate gut, marbled pearly and doorknob-fat

Growing skinny and scrawnier everyday
And longer and with a longer face
My daughter, now interested in shadows
Now interested in the grate

16. On the twentieth day finds a new crate waiting for us at the threshold

17. And ten more cans on the thirtieth day.
And a t-shirt folded on top

18. And now she is climbing up and down the fire escape with cans in the skirt of her t-shirt, and there are cans tucked in the shoulders and shadows of all the disused, disallowed vents, and in the shadow of a cloud and in the blinding burst of a sunray finding a tarry puddle and turning it dazzling, and the glint of the cans is dancing all around her on the roof, she's like a Hindu goddess, a

magic baby, a grown-up girl, and each ray of light leaves and comes to her, and she is many limbs, bountiful, and she is climbing up and down the fire escape, up and down the building and into the light.

19. In the days of her bounty we get drunk, open three cans at a time, syrup on our faces, every stuff is packed in something wet, we're stacking it all up in the hall and we can hear the rats out there at night like tin cars whistling in a chute but we don't take any of it into my office we keep my office black plastic warm and dry.

20. Now my daughter is too big to sleep on top of the drives. She sleeps under the desk of our Interlocutor, with her knees in her chest. She stands in the open doorway on the night of a day so deep into counting that we have lost count, the night our Interlocutor returns and I roll out his chair for him, and settle the earphones onto his head, my fingers remembering the ritual, but then he rips off the earphones and strides out of my office and into the hall, and as he strides away he turns around, and as he turns around he picks up my daughter by her armpits and swings her towards the door at the end of the hallway.

21. And my first thought is that he is going to hurl her out the door and into the freezing night of freefall, and

into the huge black embrace of death waiting to catch her, but then I realize he is going to take her with him, and then I realize he is going to take her away.

22. I shriek and I fly as a plane of shrieking to the doorway, I close around the escape and engulf it, fire down, I leap from my first to my last cell, I narrow as I knife I plummet like a bullet, bullet-eyed and rat-eyed and canny, and I hit the pavement back into my feet and my gaze catches and leaps but I can see nothing not even the engine firing and punching the air as the nightcolored vehicle leaps away, a steer or a stallion or a stag.

Then I fall back against the rough wall, with one hand on the first rung of the escape, my head knocks on the wall and then I sink, my head between my knees, and then I wait for death to find me, because he knows where to find me, I'm all spelled out like writing on this wall for anyone who had a mask on to look through to read me with.

23. But by morning I'm still unread. I climb like a rat back up the escape and wait like a rat inside the doorway. Behind me the other mama rats course in the hall, fiddle, are fastidious or anti-fastidious, they urge me on, they almost push me out the door, and when darkness falls I climb down the escape again and wait in the chute for death to find me.

24. He doesn't find me.

When dawn comes I climb back up.

25. The rats I think are eating the wiring. They are eating the information. From the Office behind me I hear a current pop, drool, drop out and come back. Everything hums and reboots audibly behind me. But I'm keeping vigil, staring into the aluminum door until I can see through it, out into blank air.

Night comes and I crawl back down the escape.

Night comes and I go steadily.

Night comes and I go weakly.

I repeat my crouch at the bottom of the escape. Finally I am top and bottom, doubled and waiting for myself, eating myself from the gut out, from the eye out, eating my own brains, my entrails, mama mama mama rat

mama mama mama

my daughter never said that

who would she learn my name from

26. and then that night comes when death arrives in his vehicle and his overcoat of undergrowth and his rat jaw like mice underwater like flies on spit milk and he cracks open his hard vehicle and the green light of monitors spills out and he gives back my rat to me wrapped in a blanket and shivering and she vomits into my shoulder and I hold her to my chest I bang my forehead again and again against the knee of the rat I bang my cheek against his shoe I bang my mouth against the running board as it pulls away I'm so happy so happy to have my rat back I have my rat back and I rock and I rock and I rock my dear rat

The Warm Mouth

WARM MOUTH: Chinscraper, why are you lying there in the road with your jaw shoved back your brain and your guts blown out as if you'd tried to swallow the highway?

Chinscraper: Warm Mouth, I used to make my way along the median strips and trashy shoulders, my head in the vinyl noose of a six-pack, pop-tabs gilding my teeth. I could steal the grease off a Taco John bag. Styrofoam was my bread. Oh, how far that good life seems from me now, laid out in this attitude of supplication, my head smashed in by a speeding Jeep!

Warm Mouth: Truly I feel for you, Chinscraper, for I am also alone this night. Climb into my warm mouth and we will investigate the night together.

WARM MOUTH: Kneescraper, why do you sit so still on that swollen chair which seems to breathe and groan all around you as if to swallow your small self?

Kneescraper: It's not a chair it's my grandmother's body. Don't worry, she's not dead, just sleeping, and below her is the wheelchair, but you can't see it for her girth. Maybe you've seen us neck deep in traffic or working our way across intersections like a fucked-up beetle, an evolutionary no-go, me in her lap and the motor straining to scoot us through the exhaust fumes with our groceries swinging from the arms: two-liters, sno-balls, turkey jerkey. She told me not to leave her but the night is so interesting with traintracks crisscrossing it like a gameboard and gilt-bellied delivery trucks slithering up to the gas stations. It's so hard to keep my promise!

Warm Mouth: Kneescraper, I too am curious about this night and so is my friend Chinscraper. Climb up in my warm mouth and we will investigate the night together.

WARM MOUTH: Bentneck, why are you lying between the bed and the wall, stuffed into a few inches narrower than a grave, when the whole night spreads out dazzlingly beyond the Wooden Indian?

Bentneck: Do I look pretty? It's hard to speak twisted up like this. My mother brings me here to meet men. They like me in my princess nightie and sometimes I do a few ballet steps from my Barbie DVD. Afterwards I get a treat—a Slurpee, and I can choose the color. I hardly ever drink it all before I fall asleep. Everything is not always very nice for me but eventually it is over. Tonight was different, though at first it was the same. And now I'm shoved down between the bed and the wall with all these carpet fibers up my nose and something wet on my head and my hair's not very clean.

Warm Mouth: Bentneck, we are also dirty, smashed up, bored, curious and thirsty. Get up from under that bed, bad girl. Climb up into my warm mouth and we will investigate the night together.

Bentneck: From now on, I will be called Beauty, for I will narrate this tale. That night, the Warm Mouth conducted similar interviews with a shot up dog, the suppurating shinbone of a horse, and a blue egg impaled on a stick. All climbed up into the Warm Mouth until its lower lip ballooned like a bullfrog's and it grew harder and harder to move around. The stinking troupe tried to make camp on the walkway outside the public library, but hinges and bolts, bottle glass and the plastic remains of a cheap pair of sunglasses littered the ground, irritating the Warm Mouth's skin and threatening to pierce its distended lip.

Warm Mouth: Ow!

Chinscraper: Ow!

Kneescraper: Owl!

Bentneck: Wowl!

Dog: Bowel Wowel!

Wound: Yowl!

Egg: Buy a vowel!

Bentneck: Ach, nothing's free! Life's a peep show, not a look-see!

Bentneck: So they continued on. They came upon a shipwrecked motel in which people were sleeping behind blinds pinched or rifled or skewed in a pointed, irregular semaphore.

Kneescraper: What does it signal? What can it mean? This pattern in the blinds and shades. This blind pattern. And how a gunshot's made a sunburst of the cashier's booth.

Wound: You can't make a pattern without shattering a few pasterns.

Dog: But not a very large gauge. And the cashier's long since gone away. No cash changing hands here. These people are on the squat.

Egg: You can't make a cat without swallowing a canary. You can't make a Gatsby without firing a few gats.

Chinscraper: Tell you what. I'm as worn out as a lobby rug. I'm falling apart here. Laid out flat. You can't make a catcall without catching a few winks.

Bentneck: Just then they detected a spray of light behind the rightmost room. They pressed closer to the glass, nearly bursting their viscous vehicle, peered through a chink in the blinds, and found themselves looking over the shoulder of a young man who was smoking and playing a boxing game on the TV. The room was bare and worn, but the troupe still thought it would be very nice to be inside lounging on the couch playing a boxing game instead of hunched up against the wall of a motel that looked ready to sink right through the ground. That is, it would be better to sink with the motel than fall in after it.

ALL: Sink Hole

Whack a mole

Bitch and moan

All roll home

We need the sink

We got the hole

We got the rust

We need the blood

We got the broke

We need the mold

All roll home, all roll home

A hole that will take

What we pour down its throat

At the end of the day

When daddy's come home

Listen honey it's been sweet

But I got honey of my own

I'm shunting it off

From a hole in my gut

I've got jars of the stuff

I've got problems of my own

Bentneck: But now you've got only me. Byoo-tee.

Bentneck: They were lost in this harmony when the young man relit his pipe and then, in a single motion, jumped up and swung around. He yanked at the blinds and peered out into the street. Then he pulled the blinds down so hard that they gave way from the ceiling on the right, exposing half the room. He went out of view and came back, tugging at his lower lip and rubbing at his gum.

YOUNG MAN:

Think and think

Thunk and thunk

Trunk and glove

Land the punch

Bury the pitch

Meat on meat

Whore on whore

Slunk and strove

Strunk and White

Struck and struck out

White light from light

Flight from white flight

Trove, trove

Soul's trove

What God through me Hove

The bad night I was born

& became a lug

-Nut in this case

Historee.

 Locked up with the screws and the bolts.

Bentneck: But now you've got only me. Byootee.

BENTNECK: At that, finally, he looked down and saw
them: some roadkill, a starving boy, a murdered girl,
a shot-up dog, the suppurating shinbone and the impaled egg all tucked up inside the Warm Mouth, which
was stretched so thin it was nearly transparent, a clear
fluid traced with pus seeping from one corner. They all
blinked at the young man through their wounds, and
their shattered and cramped limbs shifted wetly. Then
they all started talking at once, making a sound like an
upended graveyard or circular blade.

(All make a sound like an upended graveyard or a
circular blade.)

Bentneck: The young man clutched at his own rubbery face and then he screamed, though it sounded more like a croak. Then he crashed out through the thin door and past them into the night, which was starting to go a little grey at the seams as if it had been washed too much.

Bentneck: Chinscraper, Kneescraper, Beauty, the shot-up dog, the shinbone, the impaled egg and the Warm Mouth were startled to find before them the very sight they had fantasized: an open door. They dragged themselves inside and sat on the couch. They attempted to manipulate the controls of the boxing game. Then they closed the broken door and the broken blinds as best they could and dropped off into a noisesome sleep.

(All make barnyard noises.)

Bentneck: Meanwhile day was dawning. The young man had run for a few blocks but was quickly winded. He climbed up onto a porch he knew and curled up under the remains of a swing which was hanging by one chain and made a kind of canted roof. As the day grew hotter the heat roused him from his cramped slumber, and he got up and banged on the door. He told his friend about his vision:

Young Man: I saw into the heart of me, I saw, like, into the heart of me, I saw beneath my, skin. I saw back into the, back of time, I saw like, out through the back of me, back through a hole in the skull of me, shot through a mouth in my skin, my life, like it had happened to me, the life, like, under my skin. And everything that would happen to me and everything I'd done like it had happened to me.

Bentneck: His friend gave him a bump on credit, but also laughed at him

Friend: Yeah man, but where's the gun and where's the stash? Where's the gun and where's the stash? Is it nestled up inside the shinbone of a horse, or sleeping in a smashed egg or is it stuffed up in a murdered eight-year-old's cunt? You better get your ass back over there if you love your life. Ash and stash, gash and snatch, love and life, cunt and gut, gun and gas. Run back. Run back.

Bentneck: Did he love his life? The young man did not ask himself this question. He jumped up like a man in reverse and moved backwards through the streets to the motel, all the way tilting away from it. He moved like rewound footage. He moved like across the moon. In this way he slowly slowly reached the door that he had fled. He could hear the video game cycling through its start-up screens. He could smell a morgue with broken air conditioning, a rifled grave, roadkill, a suppurating wound, a stiffening body, a room full of sweat and sex, an unwashed child. He knew and recognized each of these smells. Perhaps he was not such a young young man. Plus an ooze was trickling all around his sneakers, green and foul, threaded with black. With held breath he tipped open the door.

Bentneck: What he saw inside was a burst spectacle, a room filled with stinking pus, flaps of skin and tissue driven into the walls, a room which pulsed and seemed to be digesting a horrible gallimaufry, the fur, bones, and innards of an animal rotted beyond recognition, a boy so skinny his ribs, wrists and legbones had finally splintered through his flesh, a girl with bulging eyes and a wrung neck, a peltless dog whose every muscle was being slowly worked from the bone, a suppurating wound without a body left to speak of, bits of shell, tooth, hair, tongue, claw, and fat bobbing and resurfacing in the fuming fluid which bathed everything, bathed even his own eyes. Then he closed his eyes, opened his mouth, and he took it all into his mouth, the room and the world, the causes and their outcomes, the couch and the game, the gun and the stash, the fix and the flesh, the anger and the relief, the hope and the violence, the illusions of adulthood, chief among which is childhood, the growth and the decay, the decay and the rot, he took it into his mouth until his mouth was warm and leaked a little and bulged at the lip like a piteous frog's.

This is Beauty speaking, with my warm mouth.

Acknowledgements

These stories appeared or will shortly appear in the following anthologies and journals.

"The Warm Mouth." *My Mother She Killed Me, My Father He Ate Me: Forty New Fairy Tales.* (New York: Penguin, September, 2010)

"Salamandrine, My Kid." *Fairy Tale Review* (Fall, 2009)

"Tumor Flats." Birkensnake (Fall, 2009)

"My Rat." *Paraspheres2.* Omnidawn. (forthcoming)

"Mothers Over Lambs." *Tammy* (Winter, 2010)

Excerpts from "Charisma." *Gulf Coast* (forthcoming) and *Propeller* (2010)

"The Bottle" *Booth Magazine* (2010)

"Welcome a Revolution." *Lamination Colony* (2010)

About the Author

Joyelle McSweeney is the author of *Percussion Grenade*, poems and a play from Fence (2012); the hybrid novels *Flet* (Fence Books, 2007) and *Nylund the Sarcographer* (Tarpaulin Sky Press, 2007); and the poetry books *The Commandrine and Other Poems* (Fence, 2004) and *The Red Bird* (Winner of the Fence Modern Series Prize; Fence Books, 2001). She is co-founder and publisher of Action Books and *Action, Yes*, a press and web-journal for international writing and hybrid forms. She teaches at the University of Notre Dame and lives in Mishawaka, Indiana with her husband and daughters.

TARPAULIN SKY PRESS
Current & Forthcoming Titles

FULL-LENGTH BOOKS

Jenny Boully, *[one love affair]**

Jenny Boully, *not merely because of the unknown that was stalking toward them*

Ana Božičević, *Stars of the Night Commute*

Traci O Connor, *Recipes for Endangered Species*

Mark Cunningham, *Body Language*

Claire Donato, *Burial*

Danielle Dutton, *Attempts at a Life*

Sarah Goldstein, *Fables*

Johannes Göransson, *Entrance to a colonial pageant in which we all begin to intricate*

Johannes Göransson, *Haute Surveillance*

Noah Eli Gordon & Joshua Marie Wilkinson, *Figures for a Darkroom Voice*

Gordon Massman, *The Essential Numbers 1991 - 2008*

Joyelle McSweeney, *Nylund, The Sarcographer*

Joyelle McSweeney, *Salamandrine: 8 Gothics*

Joanna Ruocco, *Man's Companions*

Kim Gek Lin Short, *The Bugging Watch & Other Exhibits*

Kim Gek Lin Short, *China Cowboy*

Shelly Taylor, *Black-Eyed Heifer*

Max Winter, *The Pictures*

David Wolach, *Hospitalogy*

Andrew Zornoza, *Where I Stay*

CHAPBOOKS

Sandy Florian, *32 Pedals and 47 Stops*

James Haug, *Scratch*

Claire Hero, *Dollyland*

Paula Koneazny, *Installation*

Paul McCormick, *The Exotic Moods of Les Baxter*

Teresa K. Miller, *Forever No Lo*

Jeanne Morel, *That Crossing Is Not Automatic*

Andrew Michael Roberts, *Give Up*

Brandon Shimoda, *The Inland Sea*

Chad Sweeney, *A Mirror to Shatter the Hammer*

Emily Toder, *Brushes With*

G.C. Waldrep, *One Way No Exit*

&

Tarpaulin Sky Literary Journal
in print and online

www.tarpaulinsky.com